Closer than Brothers

Takaa Silvermane

A THURSTON HOWL PUBLICATIONS BOOK

ISBN 978-1-945247-05-7

CLOSER THAN BROTHERS

Copyright © 2016 by Takaa Silvermane

First Edition, 2016. All rights reserved.

A Thurston Howl Publications Book
Published by Thurston Howl Publications
Knoxville, TN

jonathan.thurstonhowlpub@gmail.com

Cover design by Harlem

Printed in the United States of America

10 9 8 7 6 5 4 3 2 1

Contents

Tending to the Garden
Thebes, Egypt - 1395 BCE

The young fox Nitzan'ziv sat in the carriage wearing nothing but his cloth undergarments and the shackles wrapped around his wrists and ankles. He looked around at the long faces of a dozen other slaves and sighed. Chains clanked on the floor, and the feral horses clopped on the road. The noise and the glaring sun prevented any rest. Hearing his stomach growl reminded him of the decent meal he had not had in days.

The cart approached a slaver's estate. Two armored men behind the cart guided the slaves off it and lined them up side-by-side. A large, rotund crocodile approached the slaves, his tail dragging sand behind him.

"Lord Ab'si," a guard called out, "We leave these pieces of property to you, sir."

"That will do," Ab'si replied with a raspy voice.

Nitzan looked up at the guards and Ab'si. He saw the cart rider leave the slaves. Ab'si stood at the end of the line and scanned each one from head to toe, occasionally making a curious hum or a grunt. Nitzan lowered his head to avoid eye contact with the intimidating slaver. As he made his way to Nitzan, he stopped.

"What have we here?" Ab'si asked. Nitzan kept his head down, only looking at the croc's scaly sandal-clad feet. "Look at me when I'm talking to you, boy." He gave the boy a firm smack in the face, though he did not leave a bruise. The young fox had heard stories of the master's brutality toward his slaves.

Shaking, Nitzan raised his head, revealing his baby blue eyes and long, unkempt, dark brown hair. He saw the crocodile smirk at him. "That's better. What's your name, boy?" asked the slaver. His furrowed brow struck even more fear into the fox.

"N-Nitzan, sir," the fox answered. "My name is Nitzan." He was a rodent compared to Ab'si.

"Interesting," Ab'si said. "Nitzan, hmm? Like a flower? Why, boy?" The lizard crossed his arms and turned his snout up at the boy.

"I don't—" Nitzan began to reply.

"Why that name?"

"My parents thought that—"

"It was a rhetorical question! Foolish boy," he said as he felt Nitzan's toned biceps and squeezed his forearms. He then pressed a hand against the boy's firm stomach. "Hmm."

Ab'si continued down the line, skimming through the dirt-covered furs, some stronger-looking than others. He made the occasional hum and nod as he looked at the slaves.

Nitzan peeked over at him and saw him cup one of the canine slave's breasts in his hands. Her legs shook as he touched her. She whimpered as she shut her eyes.

"Ah, yes—so firm and mature. She will do nicely," he said as he licked his snout, a lustful hum coming from his mouth. "Guards!" He snapped his fingers as two large guards came behind her and grabbed her arms. "Have her ready for me in my quarters."

"What?" she replied with wide eyes. "Please, I…no, please!" she protested as the guards carried her off. "Please, stop! Someone, help!" Her voice trailed off as she grunted and struggled. They dragged her into the estate.

"Now then," Ab'si said. "I am Ajit-Ab'sichike. But you all will call me master, as that is what I am." He walked along the line as he spoke. Hearing his footsteps, the others trembled, hoping he wouldn't stop in front of them.

"Now, if you do what you're told, you will have no issues. For those that want to refuse and rebel, or don't meet the standards of the rest, there *will* be consequences."

He snapped his fingers again, and more guards surrounded the slaves, all of them in clanky, shiny armor to look more intimidating.

"Follow my men, and they will show you where you rest," Ab'si said.

Nitzan and the others turned to the right, in the direction of the guards. The guards led them to a dingy and less appealing building near his estate.

Nitzan felt a scaly hand on his shoulder stop him as the others continued. The sounds of shackles and chains soon faded in Nitzan's ears.

"Come with me, boy," Ab'si said in a quieter tone. Nitzan looked up at his menacing grin. "I have a better place for you."

Ab'si led him into the estate. Nitzan looked around at the elegant décor. He saw sword and shield racks. The rug felt soft on his bare feet. The fragrance of hyacinth and lilac filled his nose. He could also hear a sitar playing in another room.

"Kheti!" Ab'si bellowed. "Kheti? Where are you? Come here!"

Soon a young green crocodile with a black stripe running down from the top of his head approached. He wore a small black cape that went down to his upper back, and a pair of loose brown silk pants. He was taller and more toned than Nitzan.

"Hello, father," he said as he rubbed his caramel eyes. "Did you call for me?"

"Introduce yourself, slave," Ab'si said as he pushed the fox into Kheti.

"I-I am Nitzan, sir," he greeted with a bow.

"If you're going to greet your superior, you ought to bow properly, no?" Kheti replied.

"Get down, boy." Ab'si pushed Nitzan down to his knees. "Now, greet my son properly." He pushed the fox's head to the floor, the young one's snout touching the carpet.

"My name is Nitzan, sir," he repeated, only able to look at the croc's scaly feet.

"Now, get up," the father demanded, yanking Nitzan up by his arm. "Kheti, this is your new slave. I'm going to…clean him up." Nitzan looked up at Kheti and Ab'si as the elder crocodile motioned toward a mouse servant. "See to it that he is cleaned up," he told the servant as he tugged at the fox's hair. "And do give him a trim, would you?" The mouse bowed politely at Ab'si, and took Nitzan away from them.

"You are a lucky one, child," the mouse whispered. "I have heard that he is unlike his father." The fox stayed silent. "I have never worked for him myself, though. I've heard he rarely punishes his slaves, or even calls them such." Hearing what the mouse said in such a warm tone helped Nitzan's tense muscles relax. A small smile curled on the side of his mouth.

As they made their way to the bathing area, the mouse sat Nitzan on a stool. He looked around at the room. There were pieces of cloth draped on the walls, and clothes hanging upon mannequins. In the mouse's hands, Nitzan saw a purple cloth with a string tied to it.

"Here," the mouse said as he tugged at the fox's underclothes, "Let's get this on." He untied Nitzan's underclothes, and tossed them to the side. The cloth that the mouse put on the fox felt like soft cotton.

"Do they all wear these?" Nitzan asked, brushing the soft cloth through his fingers.

"Not all," he replied, and shook his head. "The male slaves would wear nothing but a white cloth, while the female slaves would wear a white slit skirt that went to the knee and a wrap that covered their chest; Ab'si's "special" slave wouldn't wear a chest wrap. You, however, would wear a purple cloth. This breechcloth is a symbol of honor—as they call it—for becoming the prince's first slave."

"I'm his first slave?" the fox asked with a raised eyebrow. "I've never heard of that. Why hasn't he had others? Is that normal?"

"I suppose it is for Master Ab'si. He believed that Kheti wasn't ready for that type of responsibility. He is 21 years old now; he won't be young forever, though. The master wants his son to learn responsibility. He is the heir to the estate."

"This seems...more like a death sentence," Nitzan said as he lowered his head, hearing the snipping of the scissors at his hair.

"Well it's like Ab'si says to the other slaves: do as you're told, and there won't be trouble. Oh...I'm Devadas."

"A pleasure, Devadas." Nitzan smiled as the mouse continued to cut his hair. "Is there a reason I needed my hair cut?"

"To Ab'si, unkempt or long hair was a sign of free will, which is one thing he wanted to break instantly." He finished cutting Nitzan's hair. "There. Go see for yourself."

Nitzan went over to a small elevated pool of water, and saw his reflection, his hair now cut short. A tear dropped into the water, causing a slow ripple. After the ripple, he saw a reflection of his father and mother—a bigger fox with brown hair and blue eyes, and a more feminine fox with blue eyes and blonde hair.

"I miss them." He splashed the water. He then saw Devadas's reflection standing next to him.

"I understand, Nitzan," the mouse replied.

"How could you?" he glared at Devadas, and sat back on the stool. "You are a servant, not a slave, right? You get payment for what you do."

"I was taken from my parents when I was your age. The men struck them down when they tried to rescue me. That was ten years ago."

Nitzan looked down, struck with silence.

"It's okay," Devadas continued. "This is my life now. I may not be happy, but I am...content."

"You said that I was lucky to be Kheti's special slave." He looked at the mouse. "What do you mean? He seemed pretty strict when I met him, telling me to bow properly."

"Well, for one, he hasn't beaten any of the slaves before." Devadas shrugged and chuckled.

"Oh, so he's not abusive?" Nitzan raised an eyebrow and chuckled in response. "Good to know." The mouse brushed off the stray hairs from Nitzan's shoulders. "He's always kept his distance from the slaves."

"Hurry up!" Ab'si shouted from behind the door. Nitzan yipped softly, and jumped from his stool. "What is taking so long?"

"You better go," Devadas said as he grabbed a broom. "Not wise to keep him waiting. Don't talk back, and do what they tell you, and you'll be fine." He began sweeping up Nitzan's hair. "Go!"

Nitzan rushed to the door and opened it. The croc grabbed the fox's arm and dragged him away.

"It's about damned time you came out," he said as he glared down at the boy. As they got to Kheti's room, Ab'si tossed him in, as Nitzan saw Kheti fix his cape. "He's in your care now." He smirked and left the two boys alone.

Nitzan looked at the doorway and saw a big, armored guard standing to the side. He looked in at the boy and Kheti with a piercing gaze.

"Finally," Kheti said with a sigh. "Father's gone. Go on, sit." He smiled at Nitzan, and sat on the bed. Nitzan nodded, and sat down next to him.

The fox's body shook as he looked down.

"Why so shaky?" Kheti tilted his head. Nitzan stayed silent. "I asked you a question, slave. You'd do well to answer your master."

"You," Nitzan said with a soft tone. He looked at the young croc.

"Me?" he asked as he tilted his head to the other side. "What do you mean?"

"You—you resemble your father. He…" He braced himself for a scolding or a beating, and then he jumped as he heard whip cracks and screams in the hall.

"Look, I'm not my father, alright? The apple falls far from the tree—very far," Kheti said as he crossed his arms. "I'm sorry if I gave you that impression earlier. I'm not my father. I was trying to impress him. I tried, but, well…" Kheti gave Nitzan a soft smile.

Nitzan responded with a smile of his own, and nodded.

"I don't want to *own* anyone." Kheti shook his head and sighed. "You are people, not property. You are like anyone else in this world."

"Thank you," Nitzan replied.

"For what?"

"For saying that. We're people. It's…refreshing."

"It's the truth," Nitzan said with a nod. "How old are you, anyway? You look pretty strong."

"I'm 19 years old, sir."

"Really?" he replied as he felt Nitzan's biceps. "You're quite strong for your age. I'm 21, myself."

"I worked with my father since I was five. Armed men took me a year ago," Nitzan said as he looked down. He scratched his head and sighed.

"You miss them," Kheti said softly. "I know. I've seen slave children torn from their parents in the lineups. It's a terrible and cruel thing to witness. Don't worry about my father too much. You're in my care, not his." He put a hand on Nitzan's shoulder. "Stay close to me, and you'll be fine. All right?"

"Yes, sir," Nitzan nodded and smiled softly.

"Now, sleep." The croc motioned to a makeshift bed next to his. "You will need to be up bright and early in the morning."

"For what?"

"Work, of course. You're still a slave, Nitzan. While you might think so, you are no guest, nor will this be a life of complete leisure. I'll still have to put you to work. I'm sorry."

"Oh." Nitzan lowered his ears and crawled into the cramped bed.

"Besides, if my father thought you weren't working efficiently, he would see you as disposable."

"Dis…dispos—"

"He would have you killed, Nitzan. I'd rather you be alive. Come now. You need your rest." Kheti lay down on his bed. "We both have duties to tend to." Nitzan soon did the same and they went to sleep.

The next morning, Nitzan was in the garden, tending to the plants. He exhaled and wiped sweat from his forehead; the day was hot. Nitzan pulled wheat, tended to orchids and jasmine, and worked the soil. His legs shaky and his face flushed, he pressed on and finished tending to almost the entire estate garden. There was one plant, however, that he had never seen before. The long-stalked, reddish-tinged plant intrigued the fox. He picked one of its bronze leaves and sniffed it. A pungent scent filled his nose as he tilted his head. As he got ready to lick it, his hand was grabbed and the leaf was knocked away.

He looked up to see Kheti. He gave a serious and stern look, one that Nitzan hadn't seen before.

"Sir, I—" He caught a glance of Ab'si in Kheti's face as his eyebrows furrowed.

"Don't touch these, Nitzan," Kheti said as he stepped on the leaf. "You should be tending to the plants, not sniffing them, especially these."

"I'm sorry, sir." The fox looked at the forbidden plants. "What are they?"

"Castor plants," Kheti replied. "They're very poisonous when eaten, and almost always fatal." He leaned against the wall on the side of the garden. "They plague your insides quickly."

"You've seen this before?"

"It happened to a young slave like you," he stated as he looked down. "She was curious while she was tending to the gardens. She found the castor plants as they were in full bloom. She must have been hungry, because she ate one of the leaves and became extremely weak. A few days later, my father's patience was wearing thin. She was too weak and incompetent, he said. She eventually was beheaded and presented to the slaves, as an example of what happens when curiosity surpasses wits."

Nitzan leaned against the wall next to the croc.

"I wanted to give you this," Kheti said as he held out a stem of lavender. He put it behind the fox's ear.

"W-what's this for?" he felt the soft, crimson, dew-covered lavender petals, his ears twitching with curiosity.

"Just to show that I'm nicer than people think." He smiled and chuckled. "Many slaves refuse my help, out of fear of my father. Either that or my father snatches me away when I offer to help, then punishes them on my behalf. They assume that I'm him. The only thing I share with him is his blood."

"I don't think you are a bad person, sir." Nitzan smiled back at him. "Thank you for the flower." He gave a polite bow.

"And feel free to call me Kheti." He looked at the garden, and his jaw dropped. "Wow," he said. "You did all of this that fast? The sun hasn't even peaked—impressive."

"My apologies, sir," he replied. "I'll make sure to get it done sooner."

"I suppose we'll adapt to that." Kheti chuckled and smiled at the boy. "This is...wow! You're a fast little fox, aren't you?" Kheti lifted Nitzan's chin up and smiled at the fox. "It looks beautiful, Nitzan." Nitzan gave a cheerful chuckle of his own. "Go in and get yourself cleaned up. I wish to give you a tour of the pyramids." Kheti smiled and went back inside. Nitzan followed and went into a bathing room.

As Nitzan washed and cleaned himself, he thought of the little time he had spent with Kheti. He hadn't been treated so kindly when he was taken away. *I suppose Devadas was right*, he thought. *I'm luckier than most.*

After he cleaned up, he went back to Kheti's room, wearing the cloth that Devadas gave him. The door opened and the little fox peeked in nervously. "Sir—I mean, Kheti?"

"Are you ready, Nitzan?"

"I am." The fox nodded and tucked the lavender in his cloth. "I-I really like the flower."

"I'm glad to hear it," the crocodile replied. He gave a thoughtful hum as he stared at Nitzan. "Here, put these on." He gave the fox a brown open sleeveless shirt and pants that were just like Kheti's own, but blue.

"Thank you, Kheti." Nitzan put them on and looked at himself. He smiled and tugged at the pants. "They fit great."

"Good," Kheti replied with a chuckle. "Let's go."

They headed into the town and Kheti began the tour. They made their way into the bazaar. People all over announced their wares: The finest silk! Fresh fish! Beautiful pendants! The boys browsed the different stalls. Nitzan caught the savory scent of fish coming from one of the stalls. He inhaled and hummed contently. He later heard music being played in the distance. A small crowd gathered around the music, snakes clapping as they listened to the seated musician playing a pungi. After spending almost two hours on foot, Nitzan sat and leaned against a wall, massaging his feet.

"Are you okay, Nitzan?"

"I...yes, sir. I'll be fine." He looked down at his feet again, rubbing the soles.

"I doubt it." Kheti helped him up. "Come on—let's go for a ride."

The croc took Nitzan to a stable and rented them a feral drake—a wingless dragon—to ride. They spent an hour on the saddled beast. Nitzan had a smile on his face, pressed against Kheti's back as they rode. The smile left his face, however, as they trotted through an impoverished area with run-down buildings and citizens sprawled on the side of the streets.

"The Abbasid invasions have taken a toll on our homeland," said Kheti as he lowered his head. "Even our own have lost their homes, their children, their families."

As they rode, they passed a port near the Nile. As he saw the slaves being unloaded from a ship, Nitzan's ears lowered, his tail curling around his waist. Their lifeless eyes reminded the fox of the start of his new life as a slave, being pushed and dragged into line for auctioning.

The croc also glanced at the auction, then at Nitzan. "That part is over for you, Nitzan. I won't let anyone bully you like that." He picked up Nitzan's chin and gave a reassuring smile. "You're under my care." The fox smiled and nodded at him. They continued on foot. Without thought, Nitzan clung to Kheti's leathery arm like he would do to his father. He hummed as if his bigger father was there to protect him. He then immediately let go of Kheti's arm.

"My apologies." The fox backed away and bowed in shame. "I didn't mean to overstep my boundaries."

"No worries, Nitzan. I don't mind." Kheti replied, and held his arm out for Nitzan. The nervous fox latched onto his arm again, smiling.

The young fox murred and chuckled under his breath. *Perhaps Devadas was right about Kheti. Any other master would have lashed me to pieces.*

As they headed back, the sun was now west of the estate. A guard summoned Kheti.

"I'll be there in a moment. Thank you," Kheti said as the guard left. "I'll be back, Nitzan. Wait for me in my room."

Nitzan nodded and went to the estate entrance. He caught a glimpse of Ab'si talking to some guards. The large croc took hold of his whip, ready to crack it. The scared guards bowed quickly and left. Kheti then approached his father, but Nitzan couldn't hear what was said over the low blowing of the wind. As Kheti looked away from his father, Ab'si forced him to make eye contact, speaking again before letting go of Kheti's face and waving him off.

With the big croc's back turned and arms crossed, Nitzan snuck into the estate and went into Kheti's room, waiting on his little bed. He shuffled his feet on the floor and twitched his ears. Kheti eventually treaded into the room. Nitzan saw him fidgeting with his fingers.

"Kheti? Are you okay?" Nitzan tilted his head. "I saw you talking with your father."

Kheti chuckled and scratched his head. "He's always like that. He was upset that I left without someone accompanying me."

"But, I—"

"I know, but he doesn't think it's wise to have a slave with me going through the town." The crocodile looked out the window. "I saw nothing wrong with it, did you? I was just showing a friend what the town looked like. It shouldn't be all work."

Nitzan smiled at Kheti's naïveté. *Does he not know what a slave is?* He scratched his ear and sat on his own bed. "For what it's worth, sir…thank you."

Hearing that made Kheti smile. "You know; I think slaves would fare better if they had a more…personal touch added to their lives. Ah, but don't mind me and my rambling." He stood up and looked out the window, watching the sun slowly set over the working slaves.

"Well, I feel comfortable around you, sir—I mean, Kheti. Never has anyone treated me so nicely. Thank you."

"Well, any master should. You wouldn't treat a pet like a piece of trash, would you? Slave or not, I see you as a friend, Nitzan."

Nitzan's stomach tingled with butterflies. Feeling a tear in his eye, he quickly wiped it away before Kheti turned around. "I see you as a friend, as well."

"Have you ever thought that friends could do certain things…with each other?" Kheti looked away, hiding his blush.

"What do you mean?" The fox stood up and tried to see his face. "You look a little hazy, Kheti."

"Come with me," the croc responded quietly. Nitzan tilted his head. "Don't worry. You aren't in trouble."

He took the young fox's hand and led him to an area behind the estate, then held both of his hands.

"K-Kheti?" Nitzan looked up at him with his innocent, sapphire eyes.

"Do you trust me, Nitzan?" Kheti asked as he kissed his hand. Nitzan's cheeks shined bright red. "I want to know."

"I do, Kheti." Nitzan nodded and held his hands. "I trust you."

"My father made you my slave for more than just...physical tasks." He looked down and gave a soft grumble. "I get lonely at times."

"What do you mean, Kheti?"

"Nitzan, I've...I've wanted to mate you since yesterday." Kheti started to blush as he gave Nitzan's hands a light squeeze. "I'd understand if you said no. I don't want to push anything. I'll be as gentle as you wish."

"Um, Kheti, I..." He felt his pants tightening and placed one of Kheti's hands over his crotch.

"Oh." Kheti chuckled. "I'm not alone, it seems?" He scratched the back of his head. "Can we spend the night together, Nitzan?"

"K-Kheti...what if someone—"

"We're safe in this part of the garden, Nitzan. Don't worry."

The fox paused, then planted a kiss on the croc's snout. Kheti took the fox and pinned him against the wall.

Nitzan wrapped his arms around Kheti's neck and kissed him more passionately. The fox's heart started beating faster. Kheti placed his hand on Nitzan's chest, feeling his heart.

"Relax," Kheti said. "We'll take this slow. Okay, Nitzan?"

And they did. As he felt how tense Nitzan's muscles became, Kheti nuzzled the fox's neck. Nitzan's toes curled as he gave a shaky exhale. Kheti slowly kneeled down and looked up at the fox. He nuzzled at the canine's member and pulled on Nitzan's pants, sliding them down. As Kheti did the same to his own pants, leaving them in their undergarments, the croc stood up and glided a hand up and down Nitzan's crotch.

The little fox got into the rhythm, bucking into the crocodile's hand. Kheti took control and held Nitzan's hands against the wall. As he kissed the fox softly, he grinded against him, Nitzan's bulge throbbing against his own.

After moments of teasing, kissing, and grinding, Kheti removed his undergarments, kneeled down again, and removed

Nitzan's. The fox caught a whiff of the crocodile's arousal, his face feeling warm and his member throbbing more. Kheti began to lick at the fox's cock, from the base to the tip, groping Nitzan's balls. The young slave started to shake from the pleasure as the croc gave him service.

Nitzan gently put a hand on the croc's head to stop him. The fox pulled Kheti back up, turned him against the wall, and slowly went down on his own knees. His tongue met with Kheti's tip, licking upward as he looked up at the croc with half-lidded eyes. Soon enough, his maw was wrapped around the reptile's dick, slowly bobbing up and down.

The fox shifted his knees in the soft lavender, spreading his legs and stroking his own pulsating cock as he sucked. Kheti brushed a hand through Nitzan's hair and began humping in the fox's mouth, shutting his eyes as his knees buckled.

After they serviced each other and explored of each other's bodies, Nitzan exhaled deeply. His body became more relaxed. He leaned against the wall and made out with the reptile, eyes closed and arms pinned. Their hard cocks pressed against each other, spilling pre and making them slick.

Kheti picked up Nitzan's slender body, prodding the fox's tail hole with his wet cock, making him murr and moan in pleasure. Nitzan buried his face against Kheti's neck as he slowly slid inside of the tight fox. In and out, he repeated as he gradually picked up the pace. Nitzan wrapped his legs around the croc's waist and kissed on his neck.

Their sweaty bodies pressed tight against each other, the fox's cock throbbing hard against Kheti's belly. He pressed his lips against Kheti's, moaning inside his maw. Kheti responded with deep groans as he throbbed inside of Nitzan. Nitzan's body quivered and heated up with pleasure. His moans grew louder, though Kheti tried to stifle them with his kisses.

With a powerful thrust, Kheti released his warm seed inside of Nitzan, and gave a loud groan as he held the fox tight to him. As he felt himself being filled with Kheti's cum, Nitzan clenched around the crocodile's cock and shot thick ropes of his own seed all over their chests. He moaned out and tilted his head back as Kheti buried his face in Nitzan's fluffy neck fur.

They panted heavily as Kheti turned them around and leaned against the wall. Nitzan felt his legs tingle and weaken from the intense climax. He collapsed against Kheti and murred against his chest. He looked into the crocodile's amber eyes and pressed his lips against Kheti's, kissing him deeply and romantically.

"Let's get cleaned up, Nitzan," Kheti said with a smile as he slid Nitzan off his member. The fox's legs still felt weak, and he found he could barely stand. He leaned against Kheti's shoulder as the crocodile picked up their clothes and walked him inside.

After they got cleaned up, they went into the room. Nitzan lay in his makeshift bed, and Kheti lay in his.

"Would you want to sleep with me, Nitzan?" The crocodile moved over to make room.

Nitzan looked around and nodded with an enthusiastic smile. He climbed into Nitzan's bed and curled close to him. Their tails coiled together as they cuddled.

Nitzan was still a slave, but he was happier than any other. He still had duties to perform, but he didn't hesitate to do them, just so he could be with the croc at the end of the day.

"I love you, Kheti."

Agōgē-The Rite
Sparta, Greece - 423 BCE

Going into the harsh wilds with only a long brown shirt for clothing and his claws for defense, Filip began the next stage of his rite of passage. Survival being his only goal, he built himself a stick hut for shelter, hunted small animals for food, and hid in the tall, grassy areas to avoid feral beasts. After a few months passed, storms spread through the wilds. The rain, winds, and snow wore on the sticks and destroyed the hut. He knew that he would have to find shelter soon, or else he would freeze to death.

As night fell, and the weather became colder, Filip searched around for new shelter and found a cave. He grabbed some sticks and laid them in a pile. As he rubbed two rocks together, he looked at the cave entrance. He saw the blades of grass being blown by the breeze. The sparks from the igniting fire startled him, encouraging him to rub more quickly.

"Come on," he urged. "Almost there."

More sparks flew as he rubbed the rocks closer to the sticks. A minute flame grew from the sticks. He gently blew on it, causing the flame to rise steadily. Filip sighed and smiled as he sat back against the cave wall. When he heard howling, though, his smile faded. His eyes veered toward the entrance, and his ears flicked.

He held up a flaming stick and gazed into the wild. Reflecting the fire's light, a pair of eyes stared at Filip. Another pair of eyes appeared, also peering at the lion. He heard growling as the eyes blinked. It grew louder as the beasts approached, but the lion stood firm. He waved his torch, revealing the bodies of the feral drakes.

They both charged at him. Filip rolled to the right to dodge one, and then, with a grunt, he smacked the other with his torch, knocking it away. The conscious one leaped at the downed lion and pinned him to the ground. Filip, with the torch in his hand, tossed the green, scaly beast aside and whacked it on the head with his torch. As the drake fell, he railed against it a few more times, giving a forceful grunt each time. He beat the other drake too, making sure neither would stand again. He then dragged the two into the cave and tossed them into the fire.

As the days passed, he cast away his civilized nature and became more like a beast. He only thought about how to survive in the wilds. His brown mane grew out, providing more warmth for him—almost as much as the fire. A month before the end of the test, Filip left his cave to hunt again. He spotted a pair of curved beige horns. They rose as a bighorn sheep in ragged pants revealed himself, looking around. *What is he doing here*, the lion thought. *Perhaps making trouble for my hunting?* He gave his spear a tight grip and aimed at the sheep with his other hand. It landed only inches away from the bighorn.

The sheep looked down at the spear as it pointed into the ground at an angle. He then looked back at Filip. The sheep's black eyes narrowed and fixed on him. He turned toward him and charged with his horns lowered.

Filip's eyes widened as he saw how fast and aggressive the sheep was. The lion held up his hands and clashed with the sheep, grabbing his horns. He grunted, pushing the sheep as the sheep reciprocated. The sheep broke free of Filip's hold and rammed him into the wall of the cave entrance, shaking the lion and making him go limp for a split second. Filip then lifted his feet up and kicked at the sheep's midsection, knocking him down.

"Why did you attack me?" growled the lion as he panted and pinned the sheep's hooves. "Explain yourself!"

"You attacked me first, lion!" The sheep struggled and flipped the lion over, pinning his hands. "I've done nothing!"

"Well, I…I thought you would give me trouble while I was hunting." Filip stopped struggling and stepped back with a sigh.

"Hunting drakes, are you?" He let Filip go and gave a soft chuckle. "What use would I have for a drake? I am but a sheep." He walked over to the spear and plucked it from the ground, returning it to the lion. "I am Chronos," the sheep said.

As the sheep took a step closer, Filip stood up and raised his spear at him, growling again. "Keep your distance."

Chronos raised his dark hooves and stood still. "I do not mean you any harm."

"Why should I believe you? I know nothing but your name."

"I'm a sheep. You are a lion. Do you really think I'd be able to do you any harm even if I wanted to—unarmed as well?"

"I wouldn't say you are unarmed. You tried to do me harm, but…" He lowered his spear. "I am Filip." He nodded at the sheep. Filip looked up to the cloudy sky as he heard it rumbling. "It might rain soon. Would you like to stay with me? You could stay dry until the storm passes."

Chronos tilted his head at the offer. Scratching behind his curved horns, he took a moment to think and nodded. "Thank you. I would like that." Chronos smiled as Filip led him inside.

They sat in front of the fire with four pieces of drake meat roasting on sticks. Filip put his weapon against the wall in the cave.

"So why are you out here in the wilds, Chronos?" Filip grabbed a stick and took a bite of the charred meat. "And how did you learn to defend yourself?" He looked at Chronos with a curious smile. "That was impressive, I'll admit."

"My father, uh, he taught me," the sheep replied. "Many of my combat skills I learned on my own." He took a handful of grass from outside and started eating.

Filip chuckled, his ears perking up. "I wrestled with my father and brother many times. I still suspect that my brother held back, though." He chuckled and scratched his head.

"I've wrestled with my father before as well, though I doubt he held back." Chronos smirked and crossed his arms. "Why? You think you would be able to go another round?" He raised an eyebrow at the lion.

"If I weren't recovering from that last bout, I would certainly accept the offer." He rubbed his sore stomach where the sheep had rammed him.

Chronos pointed deeper within the lit cave. "What's down there?"

"Just a little arena I made," replied the lion as he looked deeper into the cave. "I train there." They stood up, and Filip led Chronos deeper into the cave, where there was more space. Chronos looked around, seeing light from torches on the walls. Filip used a stick to make a huge circle in the dry dirt ground, then tossed it aside.

"I'll admit, it is not very enjoyable when no one is here to practice with," said the lion. "Perhaps we can spar sometime."

Chronos smiled and nodded at him. "I think I would like that." He looked around at the torches and the makeshift bed near the entrance. "You really made good use of your resources."

"When you are in the wilds for a long time you start learning new things—adapting to new environments." Filip shrugged as he led the sheep back to the fire. As they ate, Filip heard the rain calming. He could see the moon peeking through the clouds and illuminating patches of grass.

"The rain might continue for a while. If you want to stay the night, you're more than welcome." Filip offered. "I thought you might like a warm fire and someplace dry to sleep." He scratched the back of his head.

"Warm fire?" repeated the sheep. "Have you not noticed that I am a sheep?" He smiled and shook his head. "Though a safe night here sounds nice." Filip smiled back and made up his bed for Chronos. "Thank you, Filip," the sheep said as he sat on the bed. "I really appreciate this."

Filip took a bucket of water from the river and put out the fire. He lay down on the cave floor, looking at the bed with a smile on his face. "Sleep well, Chronos," he whispered, closing his eyes and drifting off.

The next morning, the lion woke up to the sounds of grunts and thuds in the area where he trained. He rose and saw the bed was empty. He entered the training area and saw Chronos performing wrestling moves on a medium-sized rock. Filip raised an eyebrow. "You know," said the lion as he approached the sheep, "you might fare better if you practiced with someone that could fight back instead of rocks." Chronos tossed the rock to the side and brushed off his hooves.

"Is that an offer or a challenge?" he replied with a smirk. He rotated his wrist, cracking his bones a bit.

"Both. You did ask for another match, did you not?" The lion cracked his knuckles and grinned. "So, are you ready?" He gave a low growl and faced the sheep, assuming a fighting stance.

The sheep spread his legs apart with a sly grin. The lion fixed his eyes on the sheep, though he still felt a mild pain in his stomach. Seeing that he was in a less life-threatening situation this time, he relaxed his muscles, but kept his stance steady.

Filip collided with his opponent, pressing his head against the other's, challenging Chronos. Filip slipped behind the sheep to gain the upper hand.

"You think you are the first to try that, Filip?" Chronos said with a grunt as he hoisted the lion over his back. Filip lost balance in the sheep's grasp. "Perhaps you were right," he chuckled. "Perhaps your brother did not fight with his full strength." He kept his grip tight around Filip's arms.

The lion replied with a pained grunt. He panted as he tried to regain balance and break free of the hold. However, Chronos wrapped an arm tight around the lion's neck.

"Alright!" the lion growled reluctantly, "I submit."

"Ha!" Chronos replied as he let go of Filip, "I believe I won that match, lion." Filip coughed as he recovered from the chokehold and returned to his feet. "Are you ready for another round of humiliation?" Chronos asked with folded arms.

In an instant and without warning, Filip tackled and pinned the sheep on his back.

"I believe that match is mine, sheep." He grinned and sat on Chronos's stomach as he flexed his arms.

"I'll give you that one, Filip." He bucked the lion off and sat up as Filip rubbed the back of his sore neck where Chronos had choked him. The lion looked away for a moment.

"Chronos?" he asked as he looked at the sheep's ruffled wool. "Why are you all the way out here in the wilds?"

"I...heard about this ritual of sending young ones out into the wilds," Chronos said. "A whole year. Have you been out here for that long? I cannot imagine that it was enjoyable."

"It has been almost a year, yes." He nodded with a sigh, and held his chest for a moment. "It has been...lonely, I must admit." His ears lowered as he stared at the fire. "I must stay strong though."

"Well, you can always have company. There's nothing wrong with company, right?" Chronos replied and smiled.

"I suppose you are right." The lion nodded. "Even though we have only just met, I confess that I have enjoyed your companionship."

"I have been lonely as well." The sheep sighed. "I was...uh, a farmer's son outside of Athens. I did not find much excitement or happiness." He looked out to the entrance. "A friend of my father would tell me stories about how strong Spartans were. I suppose I, too, wanted to be strong. I came out here hoping to meet a Spartan and learn his culture. Well...I found one." Chronos gave a subtle smile.

Filip nodded and smiled in return. He stood up and fanned the flames as he threw some more sticks into the fire pit. He looked outside, enjoying the blades of grass swaying about from the breeze. As he sat down in front of the fire, he felt a pair of soft black arms wrapping around his chest.

"Um, Chronos? What are you…" Filip paused and gasped as Chronos rubbed his hooves along the lion's chest tuft.

"Spartans must show love and respect for their companions and comrades. Is that not true?" Chronos replied as Filip nodded in agreement. "Besides, as cold as it is, we could at least share warmth…or at least my warmth." That put a gentle smile on Filip's face, as Chronos felt warm already.

"I suppose you are right," the lion replied. "You…you do feel very soft." He leaned into the sheep's soft and warm wool, purring deeply. "Maybe we can finish the match later. I…I feel comfortable here." He rested in the sheep's arms as he watched some birds flying outside.

Over the following weeks, Filip and Chronos grew closer. The lion taught the sheep how to hunt and gather food; in exchange he helped Chronos make a spear and taught him how to aim. They hunted and gathered food together. At night, they wrestled—though it was less competitive and more playful. Filip also taught the sheep how to dance. Since the lion himself had two left feet, he was teaching himself as well. Saltatio was a common form of dancing among the Greeks. Even though no music played, Chronos's movements were like a blooming flower to a certain rhythm. Filip also learned how to take instruction from his fellow dancer, listening to Chronos and following through.

As he danced with the sheep, Filip looked into Chronos's eyes and felt a warmness inside of himself. The more they practiced, the more Filip became in sync with Chronos's dancing; step by step, turn by turn.

During their hunts, Filip took his spear while Chronos stayed behind him and spotted game they could take. More dangerous beasts like drakes and hawks didn't fall easily. Killing them took both of their efforts: Filip distracting the beasts and taking the brunt of their attacks, while Chronos used his own spear to fell the beasts. After their hunts, Chronos would tend to his injuries with a warm, wet cloth.

One day, Filip had a thought that made him lose focus during another wrestling match.

"Filip, are you alright?" Chronos asked as he let the lion go from behind. "You seem...off. You hardly resisted that hold. What is wrong?"

"Chronos," Filip replied, sitting in front of him with beads of sweat dripping down his face and chest. Chronos wiped his forehead with the back of his hand as Filip continued, "I've been alone in the wilds for about a year. Then, you came along. I felt...it feels good. More than good—I feel amazing. I..." The lion stood up, walked over to the fire, and sat down, legs crossed.

"Filip, what's wrong?" Chronos asked as he sat next to him. He reached over for the lion's hand, but Filip jerked away.

"I'm sorry. I—it's nothing," Filip replied, though the feel of his heart racing said otherwise. As Chronos put his hand on Filip's hand, a flushed feeling overwhelmed the lion. He let the sheep remove his hand and reveal the fabric of the tunic between his legs tenting outward. "I'm sorry," Filip said with a stoic look, "I shouldn't be...feeling like this. I—" He turned away as his cheeks turned rosy. He felt Chronos put his hand back on his hand.

"Look," Chronos said. Filip turned his head, and the sheep revealed the erection in his pants as well. "It's only natural, Filip." He started to touch the tip of Filip's bulge, making the young lion let out a soft and deep moan. "How does that feel? Should I stop?" Filip shook his head, lightly clawing at the dirt. He then reached over to Chronos's crotch and reached under his tunic, feeling his throbbing member. Chronos gave a muffled moan and blushed. "You don't have to," said the sheep as he lifted Filip's tunic. He leaned down and licked up the length of the lion's member. Filip lay on his back, clawing deeper into the dirt and moaning louder. His cock throbbed and leaked pre-cum as Chronos wrapped his muzzle around it and sucked deeply.

"C-Chronos," Filip moaned. He grabbed the sheep's horns and thrusted gently into his muzzle. "This feels...amazing." He rocked his hips in pace with Chronos's bobbing on his cock. They quickened their tempo/rhythm as Filip's groaning became louder. He growled from the pleasure and squirted more pre into the sheep's muzzle, which Chronos swallowed appreciatively.

Filip sat up and pulled the sheep off him. He lifted Chronos's tunic and stroked his dick in return, rubbing the sheep's side with his free hand, while Chronos continued stroking Filip's cock. Both of their cocks throbbing and leaking pre-cum, Filip leaned his forehead against Chronos's and panted. He felt Chronos's warm breath against his neck, his head resting against his own. Chronos started to quiver.

In the Heat of Battle
Roman Republic, Rome - 51 BCE

The broken-horned bovine sat on his hard bed, slouching over and running a hand through his short hair. Specks of sunlight fell upon his rugged face from the cell window. He looked up at the light and sighed, resting his chin on his fists. As he heard footsteps drawing near, his ears twitched. The door opened, and torchlight lit the dingy tan walls of the cell. The clunky footsteps grew louder, accompanied by a sinister chuckle.

"On your feet, Decimus," said the warden. "You're next."

Decimus looked up to the fully-armored warden, the warrior's eyes glowing amber from the light, his right eye scarred from a previous battle. He stood up and headed toward the entrance. The shackles on his wrists clanked with every step. As he walked down the corridor, the torchlight shone dimly on Decimus' broad chest, illuminating his shoulder pauldron. He glanced back at the warden leading him to the outside.

"Eyes front, warrior," commanded the warden as he nudged Decimus with his great axe. The ox turned back around and continued forward. He looked to each side; there were others like himself—caged and beaten like beasts being prepared for a slaughter.

"How many are still alive?" the ox asked as they continued forward.

"There are still a few dozen others fighting."

"Good. Has he released the lion or tiger yet?"

"I assume that he's waiting for you keep the beast company in the arena." The warden chuckled and motioned to the arena. "You always know how to give the audience a good show," Decimus replied, chuckling as he looked at the arena.

They made their way out to the Colosseum. The sunlight beamed onto the ox's face, and he shielded his eyes with his hand. As he looked around, he saw the gladiators fighting; some wielded weapons, and some were unarmed, trying to take each other's weapons.

He looked at the bloodstained ground, body parts and armor scattered about in the sand. After a deep breath, he smiled. "Ah, the sweet aroma of blood and battle," he said. His skirt blew in the gentle breeze; the wind was barely enough to stifle the sweltering heat.

He saw no beasts yet. The arena was filled with roaring; however, it wasn't from any beast, but from the excited crowd. He looked at them screaming and cheering as he captured their attention.

The men and women were on their feet, looking like starved and ravenous beasts. The ox needed no introduction, chants of "Decimus! Decimus! Decimus!" filling the arena.

Decimus charged at one of his competitors, who wielded two gladius swords. He tackled the black bear and disarmed him. The swords flew in different directions as the two scrambled at the same time to get one. The weapons were not exclusive to any one fighter; they used whatever they could pick up.

Decimus caught glimpses of the other skimpy gladiators fighting in the arena, as well as the ruling lizard, Julius Caesar, in his own private seating area, excited to see the ox in action. Decimus and the bear dueled. They clashed blades time and time again. The bear slashed at Decimus' free arm. The ox snorted as he blocked the sword. He leapt back and slashed at the bear's chest. As blood spewed, the crowd cheered, craving more. As the bear stepped back, the ox plunged his sword through his opponent's chest, pushing him to the ground. One more slash at the bear's throat for good measure.

As the bear lay dead in his own blood, Decimus looked at the others fighting. A golden-furred bull charged at Decimus with an axe. Acting fast, the ox picked up the other sword and charged at the bull. His larger horns locked with the bull's as the two snorted at each other. As he saw the bull raising his axe up, Decimus dashed to the side, swiveled behind the bull, and dug both blades into his back. Using his strength, he picked up his opponent by the blades and kicked him off, removing the blades as the bull bled out.

The life of a gladiator was not always a fruitful one. Staggering between life and death every time they stepped into the arena was what pleased the audience and kept them on their toes. They wanted blood and death. Decimus was a respected gladiator who gave his audience just that.

After he sliced another opponent's stomach and neck simultaneously, the ox waved to the audience. With his guard down, he felt a slash at his back that made him fall forward. With a split second to look back, he saw a deer charging him with a blade in hand.

The ox quickly stood up and blocked the second attack by the deer. He slashed at the deer's sword arm, though that wasn't enough to disarm him. Slashing again as the ox stepped back, the deer's attack landed lower, slicing Decimus' skirt and leaving him only in his shoulder plate and gauntlets. The ox now had to be careful, as one wrong movement could castrate him; this made the battle—and himself—harder. With an erect member, Decimus went on the defensive.

Anticipating the next attack, Decimus caught the deer's arm; however, the deer retaliated with a strike of the metal vambrace on his forearm to the ox's free shoulder. All the ox could hear was the shouting and cheering of the onlookers as the violence continued. He slashed at the deer, though the small and quick warrior proved his agility and dodged the blade. However, Decimus punched the deer's wound on his sword arm, disarming him.

As the deer held his arm and groaned, the ox smirked and threw the sword aside. As Decimus attempted another slash, the deer knocked one of the swords away and barely caught the other. Though it looked like Decimus missed, the deer's skirt fell, leaving him in his armguards. The audience laughed at the two combatants fighting in the buff.

In a desperate attempt to even the match, the deer grabbed Decimus' sword arm. Eyes locked on each other, the two warriors grunted, each trying to gain the advantage. During the struggle, Decimus saw sadness in the deer's brown eyes. Again, he heard the crowd chanting his name.

The deer's eyes lacked motivation, like he was wondering what the point in fighting was. This expression threw the ox off-guard, making him lose strength.

As they squared off, Decimus felt something poke his groin. Looking down, he noticed the deer was hard from their struggle. Under the foul stench of battle, there was a small hint of the buck's manly arousal. *I see that he's enjoying this as much as I am. Maybe even more.*

Decimus grabbed the deer's head and forced him to his knees, his black cock pressing against the cervine's muzzle.

"W-what are—" The deer looked up at the ox as his face was pressed against the big member.

"How could I pass up the chance to have my way with a handsome stag such as yourself?" Decimus rubbed his hard cock against the deer's face. Hearing shocked gasps from the crowd, the ox grinned. "Looks like they're curious about what will happen next. What do you think?"

"But, I—"

"Will you start sucking, or will I break off your antlers and gut you with them?" He grabbed the deer's antlers and grinned. "Your choice."

With Decimus waving his thick member in the deer's face, the deer looked up at him. Hesitant at first, he wrapped his muzzle around the ox's tasty member and started working it. The deer's eyes full of hatred, he groaned as he sucked.

"Don't make that face," Decimus grunted. "You want this just as much as me."

With a snort, Decimus put his hand on the deer's head. While some audience members looked disgusted, others were intrigued. There was a mixture of disgruntled groans, moans, and hums from the onlookers. The ox glanced up at Caesar, the lizard's mouth curling into a smile.

As the deer continued sucking on Decimus' cock, the ox began thrusting into his maw. He grabbed the deer's antlers again and snorted. Knowing he had the deer under his control now, the ox forced him to take as much as he could.

The ox's mind started to drift, hearing less of the audience and focusing on the deer's moaning. He loosened his grip on the deer's antlers, looking down on him with half-closed eyes.

"Slow down," Decimus said as he rubbed the deer's head fur. "We wouldn't want the show to end too early." He pulled the deer up and pressed his lips against the cervine's, rubbing the deer's thin, long, and throbbing member. He pushed his big tongue into the deer's maw. He then let his tongue explore the deer's body: his neck, to his stomach, to his cock. The ox teased him, nuzzling his pulsating member and fondling his balls.

"See? You are enjoying this, aren't you?" said the ox as he glanced at the mixed reactions of the audience. With Caesar's posture, hunched over with his chin resting on his hands and focused, he looked as if he was curious about this unusual form of entertainment.

Decimus began licking up and down the deer's pink length, still fondling his balls. He heard a moan from the buck as he continued licking and playing with his member. Eventually, he slipped the deer's cock into his maw, sucking on it slowly. Looking up at the deer, he saw his eyes half-closed, drooling with his tongue out.

Sucking on the deer's member, Decimus heard some disgusted groans from the audience; however, that didn't stop him. He slid his hands around the deer's waist onto his rump, spreading his cheeks and prodding his entrance with a finger.

"Relax yourself," the ox said as he gently pushed his finger into the deer's tight hole. The deer moaned as he did the opposite of Decimus' command and clenched. The ox continued to push into the tight passage, hoping to loosen him.

As the ox stood up, he pushed his tongue into the deer's mouth again, kissing him deeply, feeling him finally loosen up from the teasing. Whether the audience made a sound or not, Decimus only focused on the deer in front of him. He broke the kiss and looked into the deer's strong brown eyes.

"I can tell that you're ready, little warrior," said the ox, turning the deer around and prodding his hole with his thick cock. As he groaned and his cock throbbed, he spread the deer's cheeks again.

As the deer wrapped an arm around the ox's neck, Decimus forced another kiss, holding his muzzle there as their tongues intertwined. He reached around the deer and stroked him before having his way. The ox pushed his member into the deer, causing smaller warrior to moan out, his throbbing cock stretching the deer's hole.

He thrusted hard, his pre-cum making the deer's passage nice and slick. He then pulled out, turned the deer to face him, and picked him up.

"So I can see your face," he said with a menacing look as he shoved his member back into the deer and pushed his tongue into his maw to stifle the moaning.

Stimulated by the deer's small hole, Decimus thrusted faster, snorting and groaning in his maw. The deer broke the kiss to let out a breath, and moaned with pleasure. Feeling the deer cling onto him, Decimus felt the warm breath on his neck and throbbed even harder, holding him tight.

The deer's member throbbed against the ox's belly, leaking pre-cum as he started grinding along with Decimus' thrusts. The deer groaned and panted as he grabbed onto the ox's horn and tilted his head back. Moaning quicker and louder, the deer shot ropes of his spunk onto Decimus' chest.

Decimus took in the arousing scent of the deer's climax. As the ox panted more, he put a hand on the deer's back and held him tight. Panting louder, he trembled in pleasure and released a burst of his seed into the deer, making the deer lighten his grip on his horn and go limp.

The deer's eyes rolled back into his head for a moment, looking faint. He blinked and looked at the ox's amber eyes, panting. He wrapped an arm around the ox and kissed him deeply.

The moment was soon over, as Caesar signaled the warden to open the gate. Decimus heard the sound of chains rattling and the gate door opening. He looked over and heard the growling of the beast that was to fight the victor. He tossed the deer aside like trash and grabbed a sword and spear.

"One side, warrior." Decimus took a fighting stance, preparing for the beast, as the deer looked at the grin on his face and bloodlust in his eyes. He chuckled as he gripped his weapons, his tail flicking from left to right.

While the deer could barely stand, Decimus took a step closer to the unknown beast as an orange- striped hand exited the cage. With cum still on him, the ox let out a battle cry; he and tiger charged at each other. The heat of battle was what kept the ox fighting, and made him strive to survive every time.

Sparring Session
Seorabeol, South Korea - 667 CE

The monks and soldiers placed the ashes in urns to be carried up to the Taebaek Mountains. Gichoi, Daejung, and Yun Yi walked slowly with the others up the mountains; the ones that were too tired or did not wish to go stayed behind.

"Hye Lee," said Yeongsong as he opened the urn and poured the bear's ashes over the mountain, "your death will not go in vain, child. Your aid and sacrifice, along with many others, paved our way toward victory. For that, we thank you."

The other soldiers spilled the ashes of their fallen comrades as the wind spread them across the snow-covered mountainside. Yeongsong's tail twitched as he watched the floating cloud. Gichoi gazed at the ashes. He imagined them as black snow in the middle of winter, scattering along the mountain slopes. He heard the whisper of the wind as it blew coldly against his cheek. He sighed, shook his head, and walked down the mountain with his head hung low. Daejung followed him once again. They made their way to the bathhouse.

"Are you alright, Gichoi?" asked the brown tabby as they walked. "You've been quiet the whole way back."

The fox looked to the starlit sky. "Could I lie and say that I am?" He looked at Daejung, his eyes half-closed. "I know we were victorious in the end. I know it is not smart of me to dwell, but..." He sighed, hung his head, and shook it again.

The cat put his hand on the fox's shoulder. "He did what he had to do, Gichoi. We all did."

"I know, I know. We should be happy. We should be celebrating. Many of us are. This is a momentous turn for the Silla, is it not? Without their general or their capital, the Baekje are no more. But..."

As they undressed, other soldiers from the mountain started to come into the bathhouse and undress as well. Daejung could barely hear himself talk over the other soldiers' conversations and the creaking of the wooden floor as he walked. He looked at the candles and torches upon the walls.

"In the back of my mind, I worried. I worried that we wouldn't survive, Daejung," Gichoi said as he stepped into the lukewarm water, with Daejung following. "The enemy was numerous." They sat in one corner of the bath. He tilted his head and gave the cat a gentle smile.

"Remember what we learned, Gichoi," Daejung replied, putting a hand on his shoulder. "Remember the tenets: have honor and faith among your friends. I had faith that you and Yun Yi were strong enough to hold your own with the other soldiers. I was right, was I not? That is what we were taught as Hwarang." He leaned against the edge of the bath as his slim tail swayed under the water, closing his eyes.

The fox hummed and smiled at Daejung. He looked at the other soldiers relaxing and cleaning themselves, hearing their laughter and happiness. He soon closed his eyes, his tail sloshing around in the water and his ears folding backward as he submerged his muzzle halfway into the water.

Gichoi remembered a mission he had with the other three when they were all cubs. While Yeongsong was training the other Hwarang, the four snuck into a bandit camp to retrieve their master's pendant. When he had lost it, his mood had changed, as though he had lost his family.

When the four entered the camp, it was crowded with bandits. Seemingly overwhelmed, the cubs pressed on. As they tried escaping with the pendant, Daejung fell behind, and was almost killed. Gichoi, Hye Lee, and Yun Yi worked together to help Daejung escape the camp.

Once they returned to the monastery, Yeongsong was furious with them for sneaking out; noticing Daejung's injuries, however, the leopard's brow unfurrowed. He took Daejung to be healed. Distraught, Gichoi stayed with Daejung until the medic ordered him to leave.

As Gichoi meditated outside the monastery, he heard a pained grunt. Daejung hobbled over to him. Concerned at first, Gichoi invited his friend to sit with him. Daejung nodded and sat down, legs crossed and hands on his knees. The orange sun shone on the two. Hearing the cat purr, Gichoi smiled.

"Gichoi? Gichoi."

The fox opened his eyes and saw the baths almost empty, a few other soldiers in the process of leaving. He looked up at Daejung, who was smiling and fully clothed.

"Dry off, and let's go back to the monastery." The cat helped him out of the bath and handed him a cloth.

After Gichoi dried and dressed himself, they walked back to the monastery. Gichoi looked up at the starry sky. Some of the fighters went to rest and recover from the battle, while Yun Yi and others practiced their skills.

Yun Yi yawned and stretched. "I'd best get some rest. I will see you boys tomorrow." She went into her room.

Daejung looked at Hye Lee's wooden sword and scratched his head in thought.

"Hey, Gichoi," the cat called as he walked toward it, "Let us practice a little before we rest." He smiled and cracked his knuckles.

"Hmm? I am not really in the mood for—"

"Come on." He chuckled and pushed the fox's shoulder playfully. "This might make for a good distraction. How long has it been since we sparred? A month? I believe we are overdue. What do you think?" He spread his feet apart and extended his arms.

"Well, I suppose I could use the distraction," he replied with a smile. He cracked his knuckles, then spread his feet apart as well. "Okay, cat."

Daejung attacked Gichoi with a kick aimed at the head, though the fox easily blocked it with his forearm. He stepped back and countered with his own kick to the cat's jaw, which sent his opponent spinning. With a low growl, Daejung regained his balance and faced his partner again.

"Now that we've warmed up, are you ready?" Gichoi asked with a smug smile.

"Your overconfidence is showing," Daejung replied with a chuckle.

Daejung attacked the fox with a flurry of punches. His long feline tail swayed as he stayed light on his feet. Daejung followed up with a knifehand combo as Gichoi dodged and countered with a right-left hook punch, then an uppercut. Daejung dodged the hook, but the uppercut hit its mark. Since it was only a sparring session, the attacks usually made light contact.

"Keep in control, Daejung," he said as they continued. "Remember Yeongsong's words: control first, speed later."

The cat listened to his partner as he dodged and blocked. After a flurry of punches and kicks, Gichoi panted, sweat matting his fur. His movements were slowing. Daejung used this to his advantage. He kicked low and swept the fox's feet from under him, knocking him on his back. The cat swung his leg up as if he was going to stomp on the defeated vulpine. Instead, he gently placed his light brown hand on Gichoi's chest, shrugged, and chuckled. Gichoi raised an eyebrow at the cat and smirked, as Daejung released the fox.

"I win this one, my friend." He offered a hand to help the cat up. "Ready for the second round?"

"You won't win this one, Daejung," Gichoi replied as he returned to his fighting stance.

This time, the partners picked up the pace in their attacks. Daejung wore a confident look while he fought. Gichoi, however, kept a focused eye on the cat's movements. Letting his confidence get the best of him, Daejung attempted a spinning kick to Gichoi's midsection. Gichoi anticipated the kick and caught it.

On his back, Daejung looked up at the fox wide-eyed. His ears lowered in defeat as he looked away and panted. He patted Daejung's chest and sat next to him. Seeing Daejung's smile and perked ears comforted Gichoi. "Remember what I told you about your overconfidence, Daejung," said Yeongsong, making the students jump as he approached them.

"How long have you been watching, master?" Gichoi asked as he quickly stood up.

"Long enough to see you counter Daejung's spinning kick." He helped Daejung up and crossed his arms. "You have to think before you act, Daejung. Do not let your confidence cloud your judgment, or you will end up on your back again."

"Yes, master," Daejung replied as he bowed. Others in the monastery returned to their rooms to gather supplies before leaving for their homes.

"Carry on, you two," the leopard said, "I am leaving soon as well. Do not stay too late."

"Yes, sir," they both replied, and bowed to him. He nodded at them and left for his room.

"Why should we rush to leave?" Daejung said as he sat down next to his partner. "I could handle another match once everyone leaves."

"I wouldn't mind that." Gichoi sat down as well and smiled at him.

Gichoi and Daejung waited for the others to leave the monastery. Yun Yi waved to the cat and fox as she left. Others said their goodbyes as well. When the place was finally emptied, Daejung and Gichoi looked at each other and smiled.

"Are you ready, Daejung?" the fox asked as he got into his stance.

"Always ready for you, Gichoi," the cat replied as he assumed a defensive posture.

They began again. This round lasted longer than the prior two rounds. The two fought as though they were dancing together. Their moves flowed like petals in the wind, leaving them both panting.

"You know, I was thinking…" Gichoi said, catching his breath as they continued, "…about that time when we got Yeongsong's pendant back."

"Yeah, that was a great time." Daejung smiled at the recollection.

"We could have died, Daejung." Gichoi met the smile with a stoic look as they continued sparring.

"But, did we?" The corners of the cat's muzzle curled up as he let his guard down. Gichoi then grabbed Daejung's waist and took him to the floor, pinning his wrists.

"I suppose you are right. I'll admit, I enjoyed the blood rush." He shook his head and gave a soft growl.

"What brought this on, though? We were only cubs back then." Daejung raised an eyebrow as he looked up at the fox.

"I just miss those carefree times we had," he said as he got off Daejung and sat next to him. "Though now that Hye Lee is gone, it just feels…different."

"I understand if you are still upset, Gichoi." He sat up and looked at him with concerned eyes.

"It is not the only thing I was thinking about," he said as their eyes met. "At the baths, I thought about that mission. We had so much fun as cubs, and then…it just feels like we have parted in some way."

"We have duties, Gichoi." Daejung stood up and looked toward a painting: the emperor of Silla and general Yeongsong on the wall. "You have a family to go home to, as do I."

Gichoi looked at the painting too, and sighed. "You are right. We do." The fox walked to the entrance and leaned against the wall. Daejung mimicked his pose on the other side of the entrance.

The cat exhaled and looked away, catching sight of the bathhouse. He closed his eyes and smiled, rumbling softly as he crossed his arms. Curious, Gichoi tilted his head at Daejung and looked toward the baths as well, scratching his head.

"You remember when we were at the baths as cubs? And you decided that we should… compare?" Daejung asked, chuckling and blushing. "And you were such a sore loser."

"Well," he replied, "we are older now. Things have…grown now." He shrugged as his cheeks turned rosy.

"We will always have those times, Gichoi." He walked to the fox and gave a soft purr. Gichoi smiled as he wrapped an arm around the feline and closed the distance between them. Daejung nuzzled the vulpine's cheek and gazed into his amber eyes.

"To be honest, Daejung," Gichoi said, chuckling under his breath, "I was hoping we would take things further that night. But I know things are different now." Daejung felt something poke at his crotch. He looked down and saw a bulge in Gichoi's pants, causing him to blush.

"Gichoi?" He motioned down to their crotches.

Gichoi pulled away and turned around, blushing brightly. "I-I'm sorry." He rubbed his own heated cheeks. "I didn't mean to—"

"It is okay, Gichoi," the feline replied, holding his hands. "You look a little flushed, though. Are you alright?" The cat nuzzled Gichoi's hand and smiled at him. "It is not like I have not thought about it. I am willing to try it if you are, fox." He put the fox's hand on his own crotch, and Gichoi felt a throbbing bulge in Daejung's pants as well.

The fox yanked his hand away from the cat's crotch. "But we are married, Daejung!" He turned away and shook his head. "We have children. Even if I really wanted, it'd be frowned upon, Daejung."

"Nobody would have to know, Gichoi; just us. Only if you are interested, my friend. I do not want to make you do anything you are not comfortable with." He put his hand on Gichoi's shoulder.

"Well…since nobody has to know, I suppose we can distract ourselves and get rid of these…situations." The fox exhaled and looked into the cat's eyes.

Looking around and seeing nobody in sight, Gichoi began to kiss and lick Daejung's muzzle softly. He murred as he heard the calming sounds of summer bugs at night.

"Perhaps we could go to the baths?" asked the cat. "I'm sure they're empty now." He rubbed the fox's crotch and smiled.

"Before we go, you should know: I have never been intimate with another male before. I'm...inexperienced." Gichoi folded his arms and exhaled.

"I have not either. We can do this slow and steady, okay?" The cat caressed the fox's cheek and looked into his eyes. Gichoi felt a lump in his throat, and his heart skipped a beat. "Have faith in your friends. I trust you; please trust me, Gichoi?" The feline nodded as he took his hand.

"I trust you, Daejung. I always will." He smiled at the cat, and nodded. "Have faith in your friends."

They went into the vacant baths. As they disrobed each other, Daejung pressed his lips to Gichoi's again. They took off their undergarments and made their way into the water. As Daejung caressed Gichoi's cheek again, Gichoi held his hand. The fox's hand was warm, as was the rest of him. Daejung's words echoed in his head: have faith in your friends; trust me, Gichoi.

After their overnight encounter, they sat naked with their feet submerged in the water. Daejung leaned against Gichoi as the fox put an arm around him.

"That was amazing, Daejung. I have never felt that way with anyone before, even..." Before he could finish, he looked away. "Was this the right thing to do?"

"Did you think it was right, Gichoi?" He looked up at Gichoi and nuzzled his chin. "You have your family to go home to tomorrow. I do too, but this night..."

"I suppose you are right." Gichoi murred against the cat. "I may have been foolish for doing this, but I would have been even more foolish to pass up your offer."

"Would you pass up a second offer, my friend?" The cat smirked at him with a raised eyebrow.

"Like I said, I would be a fool to say no to you, Daejung." He kissed the cat and murred deeper.

"I always did enjoy hearing those sounds, Gichoi." He licked the fox's chin and smiled. "This will be our little secret. We can call it a…private sparring session."

"I think I would like that," the fox replied as his tail thumped against Daejung. "We can come here again, and go to the monastery and reconcile. Maybe a week from now, we can spar again?"

"Absolutely, my friend. Absolutely."

ᴛaking a Walk
Jeddah, Saudi Arabia - 1197 CE

"And for the final dance of the night," said the announcer on the left side of the stage, "Na'im the Joy and his lovely harem performing Jovial Flower!" He gestured to the curtain as he exited the stage.

Six female belly dancers emerged from behind the curtain. They lined up on the stage and began dancing their routine to the rhythm of the goblet drummer. They all had their hair tied in braids and wore extravagant tribal outfits adorned with golden jewelry. They then parted into two lines as a drum roll sounded.

"Here he is," said the announcer, "Na'im the Joy!"

The curtain began opening as a hand slipped through. The crowd erupted into a frenzy of excitement, cheering, and screaming before Na'im even came out. After hearing them cheer, the graceful, young giraffe took the stage. He stepped forward with his purple sash on his shoulders, along with his matching veil, headdress, and flowy pants. His eyes shone an emerald green, with his brown hair elegant and flowing long.

As more drums and other instruments joined the goblet drum, Na'im began to dance. His pudgy belly moved in unison with the rhythm, while his feet stayed as light as a feather. His body flowed like waves in an ocean as he waved his scarf around. He wore an ecstatic look upon his face as he moved. Whether it was genuine or simply for show, the audience cheered; some tried to reach for him. He teased and swayed with the front row of the audience, as they weren't allowed to touch the dancers.

As the song slowed down, Na'im did the same. He danced his way off the stage as the other dancers followed. They each picked out individuals to tease and play with for that part of the song. He spotted a muscular black bear with a white nose. The bear smiled as Na'im's eyes met his. The giraffe sashayed his way over, passing by begging audience members who groaned as they were rejected.

Na'im started dancing around the big bear, circling him. While the other audience members touched their dancers with consent, Na'im teased at the bear, keeping his hands at bay. The giraffe danced in the bear's lap, his rear facing the bear. Hearing lustful growls, Na'im allowed the bear to rub down his sides. The bear then started rubbing on his rear, his big hands creeping near the giraffe's crotch.

"Easy there," Na'im said, peering over his shoulder with a wink as he blocked the bear's hands.

He got off the bear's lap and made his way back onto the stage. The girls followed him as the music picked up its pace. Excited ululations could be heard from some of the men and women in the audience. As the dancers finished their final movements, they bowed and slipped behind the curtain. The sounds of cheering and clapping boomed throughout the room.

As the girls conversed and giggled happily about their performance, a rhinoceros praised the dancers.

"Good job, girls," he said. "You all gave a beautiful show."

"Thank you, Asif," one of them replied as they retreated to their rooms.

As Na'im went on his way to his room, Asif stopped him.

"What was that, Na'im?" he asked with crossed arms.

"What do you mean, sir?" The giraffe gave a perplexed look.

"You know exactly what, boy. What did I tell you about letting the customers touch you?" The rhino's voice became more intimidating. "You are out there to dance, not for sex. If they want that, they will have to pay for it."

"That was not sex, sir. That was just part of our routine. We—"

"I. Do not. Care." He grabbed Na'im's arm. Na'im winced. "S-sir, that hurts," he said as he tried to break free. "Just know your place. The only one that gets to touch you for free is me." He kissed the giraffe's neck and gave a soft chuckle. "Now go get cleaned up. Someone paid for the Floral Superior after the dance. Best not to keep the patron waiting."

Na'im sighed and nodded, exiting through the hall. He saw his co-worker Haifa standing at the entrance. He quickly removed his dancing attire and slipped into more casual wear: an open purple tunic and loose black slacks.

"About time you got here," she said as she gazed at the patrons. "Have another secret conversation with Asif?" She raised an eyebrow at the giraffe.

"Oh, shut up," Na'im replied with a soft chuckle. "I just want to get this over with."

"Oh, do not be like that," said the tigress as she swayed her tail. "It is almost time to close, and then we can celebrate. Think of this as a present." She nodded toward the three patrons: an overweight hippopotamus, an equally large boar, and an average-sized wolf.

"A present? I wonder which one is mine," Na'im said as they both giggled and walked over to the trio.

"The wolf is mine, boy," she whispered in his ear. He scoffed, clenched a fist, and gave her a subtle glare.

"Hello, sirs," the giraffe greeted with a halfhearted smile. "We shall be serving you tonight." The wolf nodded at the other two patrons.

"That will be 90 riyals," the vendor next to them said. The boar nodded and paid the price. "Thank you, sir, enjoy your stay."

Na'im saw the hippo lick his snout as he looked over the young giraffe's body. The boar drooled, as if he had not eaten in days. While Na'im was not attracted to certain patrons, he and all other servers had to do what they were paid for.

"Very good. Follow us, then. Right this way," Haifa said as she led them to a hallway where the rooms of service were. The vacant rooms had open doors, while the occupied rooms' doors were shut. Na'im looked around and found a vacant room.

"Ah, here we are, gentlemen," said Na'im. He led them into the luxurious room, lighting candles next to the bedside and closing the curtain windows. Haifa shut the door behind them, and they served their clients.

Two hours later, the three patrons left the room, the wolf being carried off by the hippo and boar. The three panted and were drenched in sweat, with their clothes barely back on. Na'im and Haifa had their undergarments back on. The bed was a mess and the sheets were painted with semen. Haifa wrapped her blonde hair in a bun.

"Ugh, the stench is terrible," she said, holding her nose. "I think I'll need to bathe… twice…in fire." She chuckled and scrunched her nose/muzzle.

"Thankfully, that is the last one for the night," he replied as he snatched the sheet off the bed. He tried touching as little as he could before throwing it in a basket. "I hate the Floral Superior."

"I heard, years ago, someone was cut and almost bled to death from doing the Floral Superior."

"Oh, now I know you are joking. And come now; I don't want to hear that on my birthday." Na'im stuck his tongue out.

"All right, all right. I am finished." She chuckled and gathered her clothes as well. "Let us be off. I am sure Asif is waiting."

"Go on ahead," he replied as he stood up. "I will be there soon." She nodded at him and left the room.

Na'im sat up against a wall and held his knees as he looked around the dimly lit room. He tugged at the metal collar around his neck. He remembered Asif first giving him the collar as a nine-year-old.

"What is this, Asif? Does everyone get one?" he asked.

"A new piece of jewelry. It was made especially for you," Asif replied as he put it on the giraffe's neck. "Only special kids like you can have pieces like this."

"Thank you, Asif!" He giggled and gave the rhino a hug.

"Only special kids," Na'im repeated as he shook his head. "A new piece of jewelry, he said. More like a collar for a leash." He sighed and got to his feet.

As he walked out of the room and down the hall, Na'im saw the other rooms were vacant. Most of the patrons and customers left, though a few stragglers were paying and leaving, or were drunk and being hauled out by the guards, Fahd and Fakhri.

Na'im saw Haifa and other coworkers gathered around the middle of the room. The musicians started playing a lively tune. When he looked around and he saw no sign of Asif, he smiled.

"You finally made it, boy," said the avian vendor from before. "I was hoping they didn't hurt you too much." He let out a cawing laugh.

"Caring as usual, Daud," Haifa replied, putting her hands on her hips. "*Eid mīlad sa'aīd, Na'im.*" She put her hands on Na'im's shoulders and kissed his head. "Blessings, dear. *Wa antum bi khayr!*" The others cheered as they grabbed wine and danced and partied.

After a few hours, the party settled down. Daud and Na'im started cleaning the room, picking up bottles, mugs, and other trash on the floor. Most of the partiers went to their rooms. Fahd picked up a wobbly Haifa.

"Have a good night, Na'im," she said in a slurred tone before hiccupping. "I know I will." She looked up at Fahd and giggled as she rubbed the canine's fluffy chest. He carried her off to her room.

"It looks like just us then, Daud," Na'im said as he continued sweeping the floors. "If you are tired, you should sleep."

"Nonsense, it is your night. I do not mind helping," he replied with a smile. "In fact, you should get some rest soon."

"That he should," Asif said as he came out of the back room and smiled at the bird. "Come now, Daud, you should rest. I will help Na'im clean." He snatched the broom from Daud and waved him off.

"Oh…okay. I will see you both tomorrow," Daud replied, bowing to Asif before leaving for his room.

Asif looked at Na'im with lustful eyes. He grabbed the boy by his waist and rubbed his back. Alcohol could be smelled on the rhino's breath.

"Come with me, boy," he said. "I need some release."

"Oh," Na'im replied as he looked away. "I-I'm not really—"

"Did I ask you, little whore?" Asif firmly put his hand on the giraffe's shoulder. "I do not think I did. Now be a good little boy and go into my room." He pushed Na'im toward the hall and into his room. Barely more than half the rhino's height and size, Na'im was in no position to resist. Asif gave a soft chuckle and shut the door behind them.

The next day, Na'im woke up alone in Asif's bed. His eyes had bags under them, probably due to the rhino's snoring. The giraffe limped out of bed wearing nothing but his metal collar. Na'im rubbed his rear, still sore from last night, then gathered his clothes and got dressed for the day. He pushed past the pain and walked out of the room. As he went into the main area, he saw Daud getting it ready for customers. Fahd stood at the front entrance while Fakhri stood at the entrance of the patron area.

"Good morning, Na'im," said Daud with a smile. "You are up earlier than usual. You're working the morning today?"

"You could say that," he replied with a chuckle. Na'im started preparing the tables for customers. "Did anyone else wake up yet?"

"Haifa is sleeping," Fahd replied as he leaned his side against the counter. "Not even an earthquake could wake her after our encounter." He chuckled and shrugged. "Though, it might be because she drank almost her weight, too."

A weasel came from the back room, yawning and rubbing her head.

"Good morning, Farah," Na'im greeted with a smile. "Haifa is still sleeping."

"I figured as much," she replied with a giggle as she started helping Na'im with the tables. "She drank quite a lot last night."

As Farah and the others conversed, Na'im sat at a table and looked out a window. He saw some boys around his age playing with a ball in the sun, kicking it around and giggling. The giraffe smiled at their happy-go-lucky faces, then turned back to see the coworkers still talking. He tugged at his collar and looked outside again, seeing that none of the boys had collars. He then saw a man purchasing a necklace from a vendor; he wrapped it around a woman's neck and she kissed him. Na'im sighed and rested his head in his hand. He looked back again to see the others continuing their conversation.

"It's still early," he told himself as he looked at the boys playing. "Maybe for a moment, I could…"

He stood up, keeping his eye on his co-workers, and headed toward the front door. He looked back and saw that they hadn't noticed. As he exited the inn, Na'im felt a sense of wonder. He sniffed around and caught no scents of alcohol, urine, or vomit. He inhaled deeply and exhaled deeper. The sunlight was almost blinding; he smiled though, feeling its warm rays on his face.

He heard the others playing with their ball and walked over to them.

"Hello there," he greeted, waving at them. They stopped their game as they noticed Na'im. A slender black bear with a familiar white-tipped nose waved at Na'im. "Could I perhaps join you?"

"Sure," replied the bear. "Do you know how to play?" The giraffe shook his head. "Come: we'll teach you. Itimad!" he called to his monkey friend holding the ball. The friend stood on his hand and smirked, balancing the ball on his prehensile feet. His tail then held the ball, swinging it around before finally tossing it to the bear. "Typical monkey," the bear said with a chuckle. He balanced the ball on one foot, then juggled it between his feet. "See? It's easy enough." He smiled and tossed the ball to Na'im.

Na'im held the ball and looked down at his feet. He kicked his foot out and dropped the ball. He accidentally kicked the ball away instead of upward.

"Sorry," he said, "I suppose I am not very good."

"Come now. It's only your first time," the bear replied with a smile. He picked up the ball and balanced it on his foot. "Here." He passed it to Na'im with his foot. Na'im caught it with his own foot. He gave an ecstatic gasp.

"There you go!" said the bear. Na'im juggled the ball on his own, doing it with increasing ease. He and the bear passed it back and forth. The bear took the ball and went back to the group. "Come on," he said with a smile to the giraffe.

Na'im nodded and followed the bear back to the group. He began playing and laughing like the rest of the group. However, it didn't last long; he caught a glance of Asif staring through the window of his inn.

"I...have to go now," Na'im said as he tossed the ball to Itimad.

"So soon?" Itimad replied as he passed the ball to the bear. "But we barely started."

"I know," Na'im sighed as he shook his head. "I wish I could stay longer."

"Maybe we can play another time?" asked the bear.

"I would like that." The giraffe smiled and nodded as he headed toward the inn.

"Hey!" called the bear as Na'im turned his head. "I'm Danyal."

"Na'im!"

The bear smiled and waved at the giraffe.

As he headed back inside, he bumped into Asif. The boy's smile quickly went away. He looked up at the rhino, scratching the back of his head.

"What were you doing out there?" asked the rhino as he tapped his foot on the ground.

"I was…playing?" Na'im replied in a soft tone as he looked away.

The rhino grabbed the boy's arm and pulled him into the back.

"You belong here," Asif said, letting go of the giraffe. "You do not belong out there, shirking your duties—especially not without my say-so. Do I make myself clear?" He lifted Na'im by his shirt and snorted. "I said, do I make myself clear?"

"Y-yes, sir," Na'im replied as he quivered.

"Good." Asif dropped him on his rear. Na'im looked up to the rhino, holding back tears. He ran off to his room and shut the door.

Na'im sat on his bed and covered his face with his hands. He sniffed and sobbed quietly. He looked outside the window to see a tree fully in bloom. He stood in front of the window and leaned on the ledge, then jumped as he heard a knock on his door.

"Na'im?" Haifa called as she knocked. "Are you in there?" Na'im wiped his eyes and nose quickly, composing himself.

"Come on in," he replied, sitting on his bed.

"There you are. Where have you been? Daud wanted—" She looked at the boy's puffy and reddish eyes. "Have you been crying, Na'im?" She sat next to him.

"Huh? Oh, n-no," he replied as he turned his head away from her. "It must have been something in the air; I was outside for a short time." He chuckled and smiled at her.

"Hm…well, Daud will need some help with the tables soon," she said as she stood up. "I will see you out there in a bit." She smiled softly and nodded as she left Na'im alone.

As the sun was almost at its peak, Na'im changed his clothes. He put on a blue open vest and left his room for the main area. He began setting up tables for customers. However, he saw one already sitting at a table near a window. It was the muscular black bear from before. The bear sat in his beige pants, wearing a sash around the waist, showing his big but muscled belly. He looked out the window as Farah poured him a cup of tea. The distant words "thank you" could be heard as she finished. Na'im kept an eye on the bear as he continued setting tables and placing candles upon them.

"Easy, Na'im!" Daud said as Na'im noticed that he was dripping candlewax on the table. He quickly tilted the candle upright. "Stop gawking at the customers. You might scare them away." The bird chuckled and smiled.

"He was the one I gave a special dance to, when we performed the Jovial Flower," Na'im replied as he glanced at the bear again, watching him sip his tea. "I think he might have a child."

"How would you know that? Have you been spying?" Daud nudged the giraffe.

"Earlier, I saw a bear that looked just like him." Na'im continued setting up tables, stealing discreet glances and smiling at the bear.

"Well, it is not like you can just go ask him; that would be rude. Besides, you—hey!" Before Daud could finish, Na'im was walking to the bear's table, holding a metal pitcher of tea.

"Good day, sir," the giraffe said with a smile. "Care for more tea?" As he prepared to pour, the bear held his hand up in rejection.

"Thank you, though," the bear replied. Na'im nodded and started to walk back. "One moment." Na'im smiled, then composed himself as turned around. "You look familiar. Have we met?"

"Well, I did a little dance for you," the giraffe replied with a smile. "You seemed a bit intoxicated."

"Oh, well, I…" The bear chuckled. "I probably was, though I must have been decent enough, to remember a young and lively face such as yours. Handsome as well, if I may add." The brawny customer took a sip of his tea and smiled up at him. "Na'im, if I remember it correctly?" The giraffe giggled with a blush and nodded. "I am Latif."

"A pleasure, Latif," Na'im replied with a smile, leaning against the table. "Forgive my rudeness, but do you have a son?"

"I do." Latif nodded. "Have you met him?"

"I met a bear that looked similar to you. Danyal was his name."

"Ah, yes." The bear chuckled and crossed his arms. "He told me about a nice giraffe he met this morning with…unusual neckwear." Latif peered at Na'im's collar.

"That was me." Na'im giggled and smiled. "He is a good kid. I enjoyed playing with him."

"Good to hear he is making friends." Latif returned the smile with one of his own. "He used to be a quiet one as a cub." He took a final sip, then exhaled. "Well, I suppose I have wasted enough of your time. Thank you for the chat, Na'im. If you wish, I could arrange for a day where you and my son can meet again."

"I would like that, sir. Thank you," the giraffe said as his ears perked up. "We are having an auction at the inn next week. Perhaps you can visit?"

"I think I might be able to." Latif smiled up at Na'im and placed more than just a few riyals on the table. "Should this cover it?"

"Oh, this should *more* than cover it," Na'im said, wide-eyed, "though this one is complimentary."

"Nonsense," the bear replied with a smile as he moved the money closer to Na'im. "I insist." Na'im took the tip and nodded. "You have a nice day, Na'im. Hopefully you and Danyal can meet again." He got up, nodded at Na'im, and headed for the door.

"Come again, sir," Na'im said as he waved at Latif. The bear waved back and left the inn.

Haifa and Farah approached to each side of the giraffe.

"He is quite the handsome one, no?" Farah asked, watching Latif leave.

"He sure is," Haifa answered, crossing her arms. "Quite the handsome one indeed. I would love for him to be a patron in the back rooms."

"Alright, kids," said Daud as he took the riyals from Na'im and went behind the front counter. "I think that is enough

gawking for one day, no? Leave that to the customers." They all
went back to their duties.

Two days later, as Na'im started sweeping up the floor after
a day's shift, he heard the door open. "My apologies, sir," Fahd said. "The inn is closed for
tonight."

"Oh, I was wondering if I could have a moment with one
of your workers?" asked the customer.

Na'im noticed Danyal's voice. The giraffe gasped and
turned around with an ecstatic look on his face, dropping the
broom. Danyal motioned over to Na'im and smiled. Fahd
nodded and stood out of the way. The bear walked over to the
giraffe and smiled.

"My father said you worked here?" Danyal asked as he
picked up the broom and swept a bit, then leaned it against a
table. "I'm surprised you met him here. It is very nice
looking...for a brothel." His voice had a slight tone of derision.
The bear looked around at the decorations, the beautiful
curtain patterns on the windows, and the extravagant rug
leading toward the back room. "So, do you live here?"

"In a way, yes," Na'im replied with a chuckle, setting down
some chairs for them to sit upon. "We try to keep the place
looking nice for...patrons."

"Oh, my father told me more than enough about the
whorehouses when I was barely 12." Danyal leaned back in his
chair. "How did you end up in one?"

"Asif took me in and..." Na'im shrugged. "That was it. He
raised me, and now I'm here."

"I remember seeing my father in a brothel," Danyal said,
"though he swore that he never slept with anyone there." He
laughed and put his arms on the table. "You should have seen
his face when my mother talked to him. *No, I did nothing with
them, woman*, he said. *Then why do you look sweaty and guilty?* she
asked." The bear laughed and shook his head. "She was tired of
his "sneaky ways" as she called it. She left us."

"I'm sorry. That must have been hard," Na'im said as he
looked down at the candle.

"Hey, how about we get out of here," Danyal said as he stood up. "It is a nice night."

Na'im caught a glance of Asif peeking at him from the back room. "I…cannot."

"Why not? What's wrong, Na'im?" Danyal looked at the giraffe with concerned eyes. "What are you looking at?" The bear looked over at the back room, though nobody was there. Could Na'im have been seeing things?

"Oh, I am not allowed to go without Asif's permission."

"Who is Asif?"

"The owner of this inn. My owner as well." The giraffe looked to the back again, tugging at his collar.

"Is that what that metal collar is?" Danyal touched the cold neckwear. "You are a slave?"

"I am." Na'im nodded. "A few others are too—my friend Farah and some dancers."

"Come on, you could use some fresh air." Danyal took the giraffe's hand and smiled. Na'im, though worried, didn't resist, and followed him out the door.

"I suppose I will be back soon, Fahd." Na'im chuckled, Fahd nodding at them as the giraffe left with Danyal through the front door. Na'im's smiled as they walked through the torch-lit town. Where parts weren't lit with torchlight, moonlight made up for it. Na'im looked up to the sky to see the stars, twinkling like little fireflies playing about. Few people walked about. Na'im stayed close to Danyal.

"This is the first time I have been out of the inn since…a long time ago," said the giraffe. "Well, besides this morning." He chuckled, and smiled at Danyal. "It feels…fresh."

"Fresh?" the bear repeated, and giggled. "I suppose that is one way to put it." Danyal put his hands behind his back and looked up. "I have always enjoyed nights like these. Looking at the stars, going for a walk. I have always longed to walk with someone, though."

"What about those boys you played ball with?" Na'im asked, tilting his head back as well.

"They invited me to play because I was waiting for my father to return from the bazaar. They were very friendly, though. After we finished playing, they left. I have yet to see any of them, besides Itimad from time to time. I do not really have many friends. My shyness gets in the way of that."

"My owner gets in the way of my making friends," the giraffe replied with a shrug.

"We are one of a kind, I suppose." The bear smiled warmly at Na'im and nodded. "This may seem odd, but I wish my father could buy you—not as a slave, though. Perhaps we could be friends."

"I would like that." Na'im looked to the sky, smiling. The stars looked faded and the moon shone down. "If you are serious about…I told your father about the auction at the inn. Maybe you could come in, too."

"A slave auction?" the bear asked. "You will be in it too then, right?" Danyal's ears perked up.

"I think I will be. I hope so, to be honest," Na'im replied, looking toward the town. "I hate living there. The older I become, the more I hate Asif." The giraffe sighed and shook his head. "He feeds us. I'm not sure I can say anything else nice about him." Na'im rolled up the sleeve on his shirt to reveal a bruise. "I'm *his* property, he tells me."

"He did that?" Danyal looked at the bruise with terror on his face(muzzle?). "I…had no idea. I'm sorry, Na'im. He should not put you through something like that. The fact that he owns you and does this…"

"I am *Na'im the Joy*. I am expected to have a happy demeanor. But how can one be happy with him? The other slaves hardly know of his true self." He sighed, looked at the bear, then smiled. "Thank you, Danyal. I have been holding this in for years. It feels good to finally be able to speak of it."

"We should have more of these walks," the bear said, smiling at him. "It feels nice to walk with someone."

"I agree." The giraffe started to chuckle, then laughed aloud.

"Na'im?" Danyal tilted his head as Na'im's laughter tapered off.

"For once, I feel free, Danyal." The giraffe took a deep, relaxing breath and smiled. "I feel free." Danyal smiled as well.

They continued their walk down the path. They circled around the city, heading back to the inn. On the way back, they continued to laugh and talk as Danyal told a story about his family.

"So I come home; it was pitch black outside," Danyal continued, "and she was waiting in the entrance with her arms crossed."

"What did she do?"

"She blamed my father for letting me stay out. *Every time*, she said, *you never give him any kind of shadow!*" He sat against the wall, Na'im sitting next to him and looking across the street at the inn. "Father simply chuckled. He always took the blame for me."

"He sounds like a good man. He was very nice when we met. Do you…do you think he might buy me?" Na'im fidgeted with his fingers. "Could he, if he wished?"

"He might," the bear replied with a nod. "I should be going home soon. I hope we can do this again, Na'im."

"I'm sure we will be able to." Na'im glanced away for a second, then looked at the bear. "Danyal?" The giraffe hugged Danyal, startling him.

Danyal lightly wrapped his arms around the giraffe, returning the embrace.

"I know I said it already, but…thank you for this time out. For listening. For understanding." He let go of Danyal and smiled. Danyal stopped to take in what Na'im said, then nodded back at him. The giraffe walked toward the inn, then looked back at the bear walking away from him.

As the giraffe entered the inn, he looked around and saw Fahd blowing out candles in the hanging lanterns. Asif wasn't in sight, and Na'im gave a sigh of relief. The giraffe went into his room, only to find the rhino naked on his bed, leaning his head on his hooves. He looked up at Na'im, and the giraffe saw that Asif's eyes were blood-red and unfocused.

"Sir?" Na'im looked at him as the rhino stumbled over to him, "Are you…"

"Of course I am, you stupid boy." Asif closed the door and took Na'im's arm by the shirt. "I have missed you, Na'im. Where were you?"

"You're drunk, you need to—"

"What I *need* is a nice boy to sleep with," Asif replied as he grabbed the boy by the cheeks. "I need to teach that certain boy some discipline." The drunkard's eyes filled with rage as he backhanded the defenseless Na'im. The giraffe fell to the floor, lifting a hand to his sore cheek. "You need to know your place. It's here! You are *mine!*"

Asif grabbed Na'im by the throat and threw him onto the bed. Asif tore off Na'im's shirt. His thick member aimed at Na'im like a weapon. He climbed on top of Na'im and began stripping off the rest of the giraffe's clothes.

"P-please, sir, stop!" Na'im pleaded in a weak voice. He looked up at Asif, nearly in tears. The boy swiveled to get away from the intoxicated rhino, but he was too weak. Though he continued to struggle, Asif pinned Na'im's arms above his head, then ripped off the boy's trousers. As Na'im began to protest again, his mouth was covered by Asif's big hand. The rhino began to have his way with the giraffe relentlessly. Tears fell down the boy's face from the pain of Asif's "discipline".

The next morning, Asif slept as though he were dead, his big arms wrapped around Na'im. The giraffe removed himself from the rhino's grasp and retrieved his clothes, then headed into the restroom and quickly dressed. He snuck out the window and ran into the town as if he was being chased by Asif already. While walking through the town, Na'im heard two familiar voices.

"Hurry, boy," said the first voice, "I need to get back to work soon." No doubt it was Latif.

"I'm coming, father!" Danyal replied. "Slow down."

Na'im rushed through the crowd of people, focusing on them only, getting closer to the father and son. Na'im caught sight of the burly black bear with the smaller one trailing behind.

"Danyal!" the giraffe called. Danyal turned, and before he could answer, Na'im ran up to hug him. The giraffe's breath was shaky, and tears obscured his vision.

"Na'im?" Latif replied, "What are you doing out here?" He noticed the bruise left on Na'im's cheek. "Wha- who did that? Na'im?"

"Asif, wasn't it?" Danyal asked, his nose flaring. Na'im looked down and sniffed. The young bear put his hands on Na'im's shoulders. "You will stay with us for now."

Latif nodded in agreement. The elder bear had never seen Danyal so involved with someone before.

"What if Asif—"

"If he lays another hand on you…" Latif said as he stepped forward, "…he will have me to deal with."

"Me too," Danyal added as Na'im looked up at him. "We will keep you safe, Na'im. I promise." Latif put his hands on the boys' shoulders, smiling down at them.

"Go home, son," Latif said as he nodded at Danyal. "I'll meet you both when I finish working."

"Thank you both," said Na'im as he wiped his eyes. "Thank you so much." He and Danyal walked home, waving to Latif as he waved back at them.

While walking to Danyal's home, thoughts raced through Na'im's head: What would Asif do now? How would Na'im live? Would his collar ever be removed? Given what had just happened to him though, Na'im couldn't help smiling and smiling.

"Na'im, are you okay?" The bear looked at the giraffe, his hands in his pockets.

"I'm just…happy." He chuckled and looked at Danyal.

The bear returned the smile, nodding and rumbling softly. "Well, I'm happy you found us, Na'im. We'll fix this and remove this…burden." He tugged at Na'im's collar.

"Thank you." He looked up to the baby blue sky. *So this is what it's like to have someone that cares for you? It feels good.* He walked home with Danyal to start his new life.

Dragonslayer
Yorkshire, England - 1248 CE

Wooden sword in hand, the mouse's brown eyes peered at David as they stood across each other. Oliver clenched his sword as his eyes met with the boar's. Crying out, they charged at each other, wood clashing and splinters flying.

"You seem to be getting quicker, Oli," the boar said with a smirk as they hopped away from each other. Attempting to gain the upper hand, Oliver lunged at David. The boar anticipated the attack, parrying and causing the mouse to fall over.

"Sir Adam is teaching you well, also," Oliver replied, springing back to his feet. They continued sparring for a few minutes, until David knocked Oliver's sword from his hand. With the boar's sword pointed at him, the mouse stood down. David nodded contently.

"You are getting better, Oli. There's no doubt about that." He retrieved the mouse's sword and handed it to Oliver. "But we both have much to learn."

"Oli!" an older, average-bodied mastiff called, standing tall in his iron armor. "Stop lazing about and get me my training sword." He crossed his arms, glaring at the mouse. Oliver could barely read his expression because of his dark fur and black eyes, but could tell by his gruff tone that he wasn't happy.

"Yes, Sir Jacob," Oliver replied. He handed David his wooden sword and left him alone in the courtyard of the barracks, heading back inside.

Oliver was a squire, serving his step-brother, Sir Jacob. The squire observed his knight companion and managed his equipment and weapons. Unlike the typical squire, who learned the use of weapons through hunting with his knight, Oliver sparred with David, his fellow squire.

"Where is it?" Oliver murmured as he looked over the sword racks. "Where is it?" He spotted a dingy iron sword with a light brown grip lined with gold trim. "There you are." He snatched the sword from the rack. "Looks like this might need some cleaning soon." As he scurried out of the barracks, Oliver tripped and fell, dropping the sword.

"What're you doin' down there?" asked Sir Jacob as he stood over the mouse, hands on his hips. "Get off your arse and give me my sword!"

Oliver leaped up and brushed off some dirt from the sword. "Here you are, Sir." He handed it to Sir Jacob. The knight scoffed and sheathed his sword. The dog held his bow in hand and sported a quiver on his back. With some fellow knights, Sir Jacob walked toward the entrance of the fortress.

Oliver's tail swayed as he watched. He looked at the other squires accompanying their knights. Oliver ran up to Sir Jacob and tugged at his sleeve.

"Could I...perhaps join you this time, Sir?" the mouse asked, looking at him and the other knights. Sir Jacob rolled his eyes and groaned.

"Fine, but you'd best stay out of my way, rat. Don't need you messing up another hunt." He glared at Oliver, then continued along with the other knights as Oliver followed with the squires. The knights wore simple tunics and trousers, colored shades of brown and green to conceal them.

As they exited the fortress, they approached the forest—a dense and tall wall of dark olive trees. Oliver smiled ear-to-ear as he heard the birds chirping in the distance. *My first hunt*, he thought, *how exciting!* He took a deep, quiet breath and regained his composure.

"Keep up, lad," called another knight to his squire. "Do not dally."

The knights entered the forest, their squires following at a moderate distance. Soon the knights separated, taking their squires in different directions. Oliver hopped over branches, climbed trees, and stood on boulders, all while keeping his eyes locked on Sir Jacob. He occasionally looked up to the dark tree canopies, little specks of sun poking through as branches swayed in the wind.

As the mouse followed his knight, he snapped a few twigs and leaves beneath his feet.

"Hmm?" The dog looked back and noticed it was just Oliver. "Shut up, boy," the dog whispered with a low growl. "You trying to scare them all away?"

"I'm sorry, Sir, I—"

Sir Jacob shushed Oliver and looked ahead, spotting a wild buck mere yards away. "There you are. Ah, look at the antlers on him, eh?" Sir Jacob pulled an arrow from his quiver and raised his bow. "Hold still, you stupid buck." He crept closer, aiming at the buck as it occasionally dipped its head to eat grass.

As Oliver followed, he tripped over a branch hidden under the leaves. The leaves crackled, the buck's ears twitching as its head jerked up. Sir Jacob ducked down and squinted at Oliver, his brows scrunching together. Oliver stayed still, looking up at the buck. Sir Jacob aimed again. Oliver stood back up, though leaves still crunched under his feet. The buck darted away with its tail erect.

"Oli, you twit!" Jacob groaned and clenched a fist. "You scared it off!"

"I didn't mean to—"

"Just go back to the fortress," Sir Jacob said as he waved a hand at Oliver. "Don't need you embarrassing me in front of the others. Bad enough I got you as my squire."

Oliver looked down. He stifled his urge to argue and turned back. "Don't need my help embarrassing yourself," he muttered under his breath as he walked away.

"What was that?" Jacob raised an eyebrow at Oliver.

"Nothing, Sir," Oliver replied.

The mouse made his way out of the forest, looking up at the lightly-clouded sky. His ears lowered as he looked back at the hunting grounds. He walked back to the stone fortress, hearing wood and metal clashing. The sun still lingered over the horizon. He caught sight of David and his knight, Sir Adam, facing dummy targets made of hay. The wolf unsheathed his sword.

Hearing the metal ring as it came out of the sheath made Oliver smile. *Like the beautiful tune of a lute.* He watched the two, focusing more on Sir Adam. Sir Adam plunged his sword through the target's chest and grunted. His long black hair flowed as he struck the hay.

"Keep your posture," said Sir Adam as he removed his sword. "Your turn, David."

"Yes, sir," David replied. He took a breath, spread his legs, and drew his sword. Oliver walked over to them.

"Evening, David!" the mouse greeted with a wave just as the boar attacked. His concentration broken, David nicked the side of the dummy, leaving a wedge in its torso. He dropped his sword and stumbled, the chip falling on his head. "Uh, sorry about that." The mouse chuckled and rubbed the back of his head.

"Evening, Oli!" David replied as he recovered his sword.

"Good to see you, Oliver," said Sir Adam with a nod. "Sir Jacob isn't with you?"

"I was…distracting him." Oliver chuckled and looked down. "Ruining his hunt. My apologies, though. I'll leave you to train."

"Maybe we could rest for a moment, Sir Adam?" David asked as he looked up to Adam. "I wish to talk to my friend."

Sir Adam nodded, smiling. "I shall be inside. Don't be out too late. You need your rest." He put his hand on David's shoulder, then smiled at Oliver. "Good day, Oliver." He bowed to the mouse and headed into the fortress.

"So, what's really on your mind, Oli?" David asked as he and Oliver leaned against the fortress wall.

"Squires are supposed to have proper training," Oliver responded as he watched other knights and squires sparring in the courtyard, "From his knight or some sort of mentor, right? Like how you and Sir Adam were just training. Even Sir Jacob had his father."

David nodded. "Sir Jacob trains you though, does he not? I've seen you two practice before."

"Practice?" Oliver replied. "You use that term loosely." The mouse laughed and scratched his head softly, shaking his head.

"What do you mean? You don't like training with Sir Jacob?" David tilted his head.

"He doesn't really train me." Oliver slumped down, hugged his knees, and rested his head against the wall. "He just gives false instructions to look presentable in front of the other knights. The only "training" I've gotten was from observing other knights training their squires. And with you, of course." He smiled up at the boar, then looked at the entrance. "I once overheard Sir Jacob and his father saying that I wasn't worth training."

David sat next to the mouse. "I don't believe that, Oli. You're great to train with when I'm not practicing with Sir Adam." Those words didn't lift Oliver's spirits. "What if I help you?"

"What?" Oliver raised an eyebrow at him. "You couldn't possibly—"

"Why not?" The boar sprung up and grinned. "I've had much more experience as a squire. The least I could do for a friend is pass on what I know."

"I guess you do have more experience." The mouse tapped his chin with his finger, staring ahead. "Are you sure you would be okay helping me train, as well as doing your duties? Would Sir Adam approve?" David nodded reassuringly. "I'll help you with your duties as well. Don't want you to be overwhelmed." Oliver smiled and stood up.

"Come then; let's go inside." The boar gestured toward the building. "It's getting dark."

The sun soon sank beneath the horizon. As they were about to head inside, Oliver heard people laughing as they approached the entrance. He saw the knights returning with their game dragged behind them or hoisted on their shoulders. Sir Jacob carried two rabbits by their ears in one hand. Oliver looked on and sighed.

"Come on, Oliver," David said as he put his hand on Oliver's shoulder.

The two squires went inside, walking down the wide torch-lit hallway, and passed a small chapel for the faithful. Oliver peeked in and saw Sir Adam on bended knee in front of an altar, his hands interlocked. Candles were lit on either side of the altar. A gold-embroidered red tapestry was draped over the altar. A cross stood upright with the Lord Savior tied to it. A statue of the Virgin Mother stood behind the altar.

"Hearken, O Lord," Sir Adam prayed, "...we beseech Thee to our prayers..."

The boar and mouse entered quietly so as not to disturb him. David kneeled on his knight's right side and continued praying with him. "...and deign to bless with Thy Majesty's right hand, this sword with which Thine servant desires to be girded..."

Oliver joined them, kneeling on Sir Adam's left side and praying as well. "...defense of churches, widows, orphans, and all Thy servants against the scourge of pagans, that it may be the terror and dread of all evil-doers, and that it may be just in both attack and defense."

Sir Adam opened his eyes and smiled at the boys as he stood up. "Get some rest." He tapped their shoulders with his hands. "It's late. I'll see you tomorrow, David." The wolf left the room.

"I wonder," said Oliver as he looked at Jesus on the cross. "Does He pay attention to...whelps like me?"

"Why wouldn't He?" David rose to his feet. "Our Lord listens to anyone and everyone that calls upon Him."

"I hope you're right." The mouse sighed and stood up as well.

They parted ways to rest. As Oliver lay on his haystack bed in the sleeping room, he looked up to the ceiling. *Why won't you help me?* He sighed and turned to his side. *Do you really think I would be that bad of a knight?* He slowly closed his eyes. *Maybe...* He yawned. *I'm just destined to be...a squire.* He yawned again soon drifted off into slumber.

The next day, the mouse left his room barely awake, rubbing his eyes as he walked through the fortress. After eating some bread and drinking water, he headed towards the entrance. He jumped, lifting his hands in alarm as he was greeted by David with a sword pointed at him. The boar had a sword in each hand, and shields leaned against the wall.

"Ready for a little training?" David asked with a smile, offering one of the swords.

Oliver returned the smile, nodded, and took the other sword and one of the shields. They headed out to the courtyard and faced a hay dummy. David unsheathed his sword and began thrusting at the target, letting out forceful grunts. After the boar finished, Oliver mimicked David's movements, hitting the dummy as well.

"Hey, perhaps you do train better by observance," David said, smiling and crossing his arms. Oliver nodded at him with a smile of his own. "See if you can do this," the boar said before performing a quick three-hit combination on the dummy. He stood back and nodded to the mouse. Oliver mimicked David's movements precisely. They continued taking turns attacking the target.

Soon, Oliver caught a glimpse of Sir Jacob conversing with other knights. The knights climbed upon their horses, lances firm in their grips. They stood in a line, facing wooden dummies. The dummies had targeted shields at their torsos.

The knights raised their lances. One after the other, they charged at their targets, their lances clashing into the wooden shields.

"One day, that will be us," David said as he stood next to the mouse and watched the knights. "We'll be riding on horses—maybe even fighting alongside his majesty himself."

"Maybe." Oliver smiled at David. "Let's continue."

The boys continued training with dummies. After almost an hour, took a short break, placing their shields to one side. Oliver panted and chuckled, his enthusiasm showing in his eyes. Catching his breath, David repositioned his shield onto his arm.

"Ready to face someone that can fight back?" David pointed his sword at the mouse.

Oliver held his sword in his hand and nodded to David. They charged at each other and began sparring. Clang after clang, the squires clashed swords. Fatigued from attacking the dummies, Oliver began slowing his attacks. David slowed his own movements in response.

"Getting tired I see?" the boar asked with a tilted head.

The winded Oliver looked up at him, seeing Sir Jacob in David's place. He charged at David with more tenacity. The boar gasped, barely blocking Oliver's barrage.

"Why don't...you believe...in me?" The words slipped through Oliver's mouth between pants as he attacked.

"Oli!" David grunted, looking into the mouse's eyes.

The black in Oliver's eyes almost doubled in size, and his nose flared. His attacks became fiercer and his cries angrier.

"Oli, relax!" David parried an attack and knocked Oliver's sword out of his hand. "Calm yourself, friend." He restrained the mouse, grabbing his arms. "I'm not Sir Jacob."

The younger squire panted, his eyes returning to normal as he looked up at David. "I...I'm sorry David," he said as he relaxed his stance. "I got carried away."

"Come on," David replied, sheathing his sword. He handed Oliver his own sword as he continued speaking, "Let's go to the stables."

As they walked over to the stables, a strong odor of horse droppings filled the poor mouse's nose. He groaned, turned his head up, and held his nose.

"They must have been eating the extra feed again," Oliver said as he saw the bag and food all over the ground. "They should make that harder to get to."

David chuckled and picked up two shovels, then handed one to Oliver. The mouse gave David a raised eyebrow, which he returned with a shrug. They began scooping the horse droppings out of the stalls and into buckets—which David was supposed to do by himself. Those buckets were taken to the edge of the forest to be dumped out.

Oliver stole quick glances at the boar. *Why do you believe in me?* He couldn't hide a puzzled expression. He petted one horse, stroking its mane softly. *Why help me through my time as a squire?*

"Oli?" David stopped sweeping as he looked at him. "Is something wrong?"

"I just..." They continued sweeping. "There has to be another way to become a knight. Maybe...maybe I could defeat those Flametongue bandits, or something?"

"You're joking?" replied the boar with a laugh. "When I said you had potential, Oli, I didn't mean you could defeat a bloody bandit group." He patted the mouse's shoulder as his laughter slowly waned. Oliver simply gave him a stern look in response. "Oliver. You aren't joking, are you?"

"I'm tired of being this way, David," he replied as he shook his head. "I know you mean well, my friend, and I truly appreciate it, but..."

"Oli, do you hear yourself? You're talking about a group of bandits, not some wild doe." They walked out of the stables and around the fortress. "These things take time, Oli." David looked at the knights. "I want to fight with them too, but we're just not ready yet. We need to be patient. Only God knows what will happen."

"That may be fine for you, David, but—" The young mouse put his shovel down, holding his head and giving a soft sigh. "I'm sorry. I just... need to think things through." He put his hand on David's shoulder. "Go on and train with Sir Adam. I'll be fine."

David looked down, but then nodded at Oliver. "Don't do anything rash, Oli. Okay?" He smiled and nudged the mouse softly before heading inside.

Oliver sat down and picked at some grass, looking toward the cyan sky. He heard thuds and grunts from knights. Peeking around the corner, he saw chips of wood flying from the dummies as they were attacked. He got up and walked around the corner, watching the knights practicing in the yard, and caught a glimpse of David. The mouse smiled, and his tail swayed as he watched his friend thrust his sword and hold up his shield; Sir Adam looked on with crossed arms and the occasional nod.

He then saw Sir Jacob, still training with his lance. Without a second thought, the mouse went back into the fortress. He went into the chapel and prayed. "...we beseech Thee to our prayers..."

His prayer was interrupted by the sound of someone running in the hall, loudly panting. A lightly-armored canine was headed to the commander's quarters, his footsteps almost quiet as he sprinted. Oliver snuck out of the chapel and down the hall toward the commander's quarters.

"Are you sure," asked the commander, "you saw them here?"

"Yes, sir knight." The courier nodded at him. "Some scouts on the mountainside, said the bandits might possibly head to York—"

The commander shut the door, making the rest of the conversation indistinct to Oliver. The mouse returned to the chapel and sat on a bench, his chin resting on his hands.

David found the mouse shortly afterward. "Oli?" he greeted, snapping Oliver out of his thoughts. "Is everything alright? I figured you might want to come train with me and Sir Adam." Oliver did not respond as he looked at the cross. "What's wrong, Oli?" The boar sat next to Oliver, wearing a look of concern.

"The Flametongue are here," Oliver replied as he stood up, "I heard a messenger talking with the commander. They're on the Dales."

"And...?" David stood as well, raising an eyebrow. "What are you planning, Oli?"

"Well..." Oliver paused as he paced back and forth. "I assume the commander will send a group up the mountain to confront them, right?"

"And...?" David stressed, crossing his arms. "You aren't thinking of going with them, are you?"

"Well, I—"

"Ah, I'm glad I found you, David," Sir Adam interrupted. "The Flametongue are hiding in a cave in the Dales. A few others and I are going to search for the cave. We need to take the battle to them before they can do our city any harm. Make haste."

"Uh, Sir Adam?" Oliver asked, scratching his head. "Could I perhaps join you on your search? I promise, I won't be in your way."

"You need to talk to Sir Jacob about that, Oliver. It is not my decision. Let's go, David." Sir Adam and David left to prepare, leaving Oliver alone.

The mouse sat down on the bench. *I suppose it wouldn't hurt to ask.* He stood up, brushed off his trousers, and left the chapel. He headed toward the room where Sir Jacob and the other knights ate. As he treaded, Oliver gripped his chest, feeling his heart race. He stopped and gulped heavily. *Straighten up, Oli. Being a sniveling coward is not what makes a knight!* He took a deep breath and continued walking toward the knight's mess hall. He saw other knights sitting and conversing around the table, but there was no sign of Sir Jacob. He tilted his head and hummed curiously, wondering where Sir Jacob might be. He searched for his knight in the courtyard, but there was no sign of him. He went back into the fortress and looked around for Sir Adam or David, but couldn't find them either.

"Could they have left already?" he asked aloud as he went into the mess hall and sat down at a table. The smell of rotting chicken from unfinished dishes filled the air. He groaned and held his breath, his cheeks puffing out.

After a few moments, he decided to take the wooden plates into the kitchen and wash them himself. He noticed the cook doing his duties, humming to himself and wagging his docked pug tail as he stirred something in a big pot. He also noticed the mask on his face, muffling his speech; rumor was that he had a drooling problem as a pup.

"Mix it up into the stew..." the cook sang in a gruff voice, "...I'll be damned if it goes right through—"

"Pardon me, sir."

"What's this?" the cook stopped stirring and looked over to the mouse. "Oh, what can I do for you, squire?"

"Have you seen Sir Jacob?"

"Aye, he should be getting ready with the other knights." the cook replied as he continued stirring while looking at Oliver. "You his squire, mouse?"

Oliver nodded. "You could use the term 'squire' loosely." He shook his head. "Thank you, sir cook." He left the cook to his duties, hearing the gruff singing resume.

The mouse went to the armory, seeing the knights dressing and arming themselves for the upcoming battle. However, he did not see Sir Jacob. He then checked his bedchamber, but no luck there either. *Could he be avoiding me?*

He sat on the bed, looking down at the floor. Sir Jacob's voice rushed through Oliver's mind: *Get off your arse! Stop lazing about, and bring me my training sword. You'd best stay out of my way.* He went back to his own bed in the squires' chamber and watched from his room as the crowd of knights departed with their squires.

"I'm not the worthless boy you think I am, Sir Jacob," he said, clenching a fist. "I'll...I'll show you, I'm not!" He left the chamber, grabbing a sword and shield from the weapon racks on the corridor wall. As he walked toward the exit to the fortress, he saw a few knights training in the courtyard. He stuck to the wall, creeping slowly toward the gate. He looked around and saw some knights still training outside the front. Opening the gate would make too much noise, so he made his way around the side and saw stacked crates and barrels. Nobody in sight, the mouse climbed and hopped over the fortress wall.

He stuck to the wall again, seeing some of the men patrolling atop the wall encircling the fortress. When they made their way to the other side, Oliver bolted toward the forest. He looked around one more time. Nobody had noticed him, and he gave a relieved chuckle.

"Okay, Oliver," he whispered to himself as he took a deep breath. "If I succeed, I will prove Sir Jacob wrong; I might be able to creep out from his shadow. If I fail…well, I suppose it just proves I was ill-equipped after all, and I'll finally be out of his way. I've made it this far." As he made his way to the drawbridge, he slinked around a corner, seeing some of the men patrolling atop the wall encircling the fortress. When they made their way to the other side, Oliver bolted toward the forest. He looked around one more time. Nobody had noticed him, and he gave a relieved chuckle.

He exhaled and looked toward the mountain range known as the Dales. Somewhere among those mountains was the Flametongue. He would have to go through the town to make his way to the Dales. He snuck a horse out of the stable and rode it through the city.

Making his way to the Dales, Oliver looked at the mountainside. The snow glimmered off the light of the sun hiding behind a tall peak. He took a moment, smiling at the beautiful view.

The mouse took a deep breath, then shook his hands and continued forward. With his claws, Oliver scaled the mountainside. He continued searching for the bandits—or even any knights, for that matter, keeping his eyes open for a cave embedded in the mountains.

After the sun rested beneath the horizon, Oliver sat down in an area that was not rocky and rested his feet. He looked up at the stars, taking in another moment of beauty. *Never thought I could see the stars like this.*

"Now where is this cave?" he asked himself as he rubbed his feet. His sensitive ears perked just then, hearing voices in the distance. He got back up and started walking over a hill. Oliver heard the conversation getting louder, then saw a couple of bandits—a scruffy rat and lion—in front of a cave entrance. He hid behind the hill and listened in.

"Yeah, chief says we are going to attack that puny town tomorrow," said one of the bandits with a raspy voice as he gave a low growl. "I would love to see those knights come at us."

"Yeah, they probably have little pigstickers for swords," said the other man. Oliver heard them laugh as they left their post. Their laughter trailed off into the distance. He peeked up and saw nobody there. The entrance was lit only by a lantern hanging above it.

"I'd best hurry," he whispered to himself. He bolted for the entrance. The passageway was lit with torches. It reeked of rotting dead animals, the stench threatening to turn his stomach. Oliver also saw dead feral drakes with flies buzzing around them. *Perhaps this cave was inhabited by drakes at some point.*

He continued deeper into the cave and saw some of the Flametongue members. Unfortunately, they spotted him as well. One pig bandit snarled at him, his features marred by an eyepatch and unsightly face.

"Intruder!" the pig shouted. "Intruder!"

Oliver drew his sword and shield. There wasn't much time to think. He had to act and react quickly. They charged at him. He parried and killed one with ease, then another.

"Keep your guard up, Oli," he told himself. "Do not hold back. Do not waver." His confidence grew as he felled the weak attackers one by one, letting out an occasional chuckle. Blood spewed from the wounds of the bandits. He went through the motions of dodging and slashing, hearing their grunts of pain. He raised his eyebrows as he looked at his bloodstained sword. "Wow. These bandits are almost as bad as Jacob." He traversed the cave, shivering from the chilly air. He panted softly as he saw bandit corpses sprawled around the cavern. The stench of death grew more prominent.

As he made his way to the end of the cave, Oliver found himself in a large, dark, open cavern, hot and damp like a spring. Oliver wiped sweat from his forehead. On three sides of the cave, torches were lit. A large horned dragon with grey scales revealed himself in the torchlight of the cave, standing tall. His large wings flapped then folded behind him.

Oliver gazed at his muscular shirtless body as he pulled at his own collar. The dragon peered at Oliver with fiery red eyes. Despite the legends, the dragon walked on two feet instead of four.

The dragon was accompanied by two equally shirtless dragonlings—a green-scaled one and a blue-scaled one—their wings folded as well. They were almost as muscular as the one in front of Oliver. The green-scaled dragonling looked at Oliver perplexedly, then at the blue-scaled dragonling.

"Chief," he said as he turned toward the adult dragon, "he looks smaller than those other knights."

"It would appear so," the chief replied as he stepped forward. "Tell me, boy, are you a knight?" Oliver shook his head. His legs shook. "Of course not, or else your legs would not be quivering like that. Look at you." The other two laughed, though they immediately stopped when their chief raised a hand. "So, boy, what is your name?"

"O…Oliver, sir," he replied. "My name is Oliver. I'm a squire." He looked at the ground, embarrassed to say his title.

"Look at me, Oliver the squire. It's rude to not make eye contact," said the dragon. As Oliver complied, he continued speaking, "I am Alistair Flametongue. You may call me Alistair. Now, let us be civil, hm?" With every step the dragon took, the mouse took a step back. "You came to my camp and killed my men. Not very polite, is it? Then again, they must not have been the most competent of men if they were beaten by a mere squire. In a way, you proved their worth. However, the question stands: why are you here? You could not have possibly thought that you could defeat me alone, could you?"

"I…wanted to become a knight. I thought this would be the quickest way to do it."

"Maybe if you had actual training/actually trained as a knight, you might stand a chance against me." The dragon drew a thin sword with an exquisite handle. He performed some movements with the sword. Oliver couldn't help but watch and admire the dragon's grace as his body glistened from the steamy air. He then sheathed his sword.

"Do you know why they call me Flametongue, squire?" Alistair asked. Oliver shook his head. Alistair then blew a huge gout of flame into the air as the other two stood back. "It is a bit difficult for knights to fight a fire-breathing dragon, is it not? However, you show a decent amount of skill. I have decided not to kill you."

"What?!" said the blue-scale. "But sir, he practically—"

Alistair held the blue-scale's maw shut. "Murdered our whole group." He chuckled. "Yes, and it showed how incompetent they were. If you wish not to be next, you will shut your roaring screamer."

"So, does this mean you are letting me go free?" Oliver asked with his ears perked up, his eyes widening.

"Not quite," the dragon replied. "You killed my men. I require some form of compensation."

"What kind of compensation do you mean?"

"You take something of mine, I take something of yours. We both walk away a little worse for wear, but alive and uninjured. Who knows, someone might witness your bravery."

"I, uh…" Oliver backed away, but bumped into the green-scaled dragonling that moved behind him. Even as dragonlings, they were still taller than Oliver.

"It has been too long since any of us have had any…release, you see. You spend one night with us, we will leave England, and you increase your chances of becoming a knight. As I have said, you have the potential. All you really need is notoriety. Or you could be stupid and refuse, and we can make this your grave. Your choice."

After hearing Alistair's threat, Oliver's heart raced. Feeling the muscled dragonling's body behind him did not help him much either. He crossed his legs to hide his excitement. Oliver smelled the one behind him and caught a whiff of arousal. The dragonling behind him pushed Oliver closer to Alistair. The three closed in on the mouse as Alistair untied Oliver's shirt

stood on each side of him and started stroking their cocks slowly. "Ready, squire?"

Oliver nodded as Alistair pinned his hands. After the blue-scale made Oliver's hole ready for Alistair, the dragon pushed his thick throbbing cock into the mouse. Oliver moaned out and bit his lip, feeling the thickness go inside him. His instinctive reaction was to tighten up, which made Alistair groan.

The dragon pulled the mouse into his lap and started thrusting deeper. The dragonlings brought their cocks closer to the Oliver and Alistair, both of them sucking each one.

As they went on for almost an hour, Oliver felt a deep tingling building up inside him as Alistair's cock throbbed even harder inside him. The mouse moaned louder and louder. He hugged onto the strong dragon as he felt the barbs lining Alistair's shaft brush up against his insides.

Those barbs sent him over the edge, and the pleasuring sensation peaked. He shot his mouse seed all over himself and Alistair. In that same moment, Alistair shot waves of his hot dragon spunk inside of him. Alistair groaned and panted into the mouse's neck. They embraced tightly as the dragonlings climaxed all over the boy and dragon.

In the end, they rested in their undergarments with each other as the dragonlings did the same.

"You sure know how to slay a dragon, boy," said Alistair.

"T-thank you, sir. That was my first time," Oliver replied with a blush.

"Was it now? Well I suppose I took something from you then." The muscled dragon chuckled and smiled. "I made a deal with you, Oliver. I've gotten what I wanted, so will you. Here." He gave a soft, pained grunt as he broke off a piece of one of the horns lining his head. "It grows back. Don't worry. You need some sort of evidence that I'm 'dead', right?" He chuckled as he and the dragonlings gathered their clothes. He turned his back on Oliver. "Good luck on your endeavors." He turned his head and looked at the mouse. "May our paths never cross again, young mouse. The outcome might not be as desired."

Oliver nodded as Alistair and the others flew through a hole in the cave.

The mouse held the horn in his hand. He got dressed and made his way out of the cave, just as some of the townspeople approached it.

"Oli!" David shouted as he ran over to hug him. "What is that in your hand?" he asked as he held the horn. "This is from a… you've slain him? You've slain the dragon?!" The others gasped.

Oliver chuckled and scratched his head. "Well, I—"

"This boy saved the town!" announced another villager. Others began praising the mouse for his apparent deed.

As they went down the mountain, Oliver could not even lie about the event, as the others kept talking over him. *Well I kept the dragon away from the city. That's what matters, right?*

Cold Embrace
Bucharest, Romania - 1597 CE

Every beginning must have an ending. My mother's thoughts on life. She used to tell me this, before she died. Others think, however, that it is their right to live in eternity, with no limitations.

I'm Stanislav Ranefoust, a member of the Ranefoust family outside Bucharest. I've always agreed with my mother's opinion on life. Our family is large, but with such disagreement, some of us were more distant than others.

Some of the members of the family fed to sustain their existence in the sun. Others did it to turn other mortals. Some would play with their food. We were a *special* kind of bat. We were born with Sanguaris, or vampirism.

While there are many other vampires in Romania, my father said that we were the only true vampires. We were the only ones born from the blood of the ancestors of Vlad the Impaler. There were many stories on how Vladimir became a vampire. The most common belief was that he was inflicted by Satan himself. No matter what the story, we were different...and dangerous to many.

Seeing as we were sons of Satan, many saw us as enemies of God. This caused hysteria in the cities. Citizens gathered garlic and wooden stakes as methods of destruction and to prevent being bitten. A small few even went so far as to decapitate heads and put them on their front door. However, that practice didn't catch on as well. While the majority took precautionary measures, some citizens didn't give in to the hysteria.

This stigma has thus been spread to even non-vampiric bats. The few of us that are not abusive of our powers have tried to socialize with mortals and prove our benevolence—to no avail. Others, like my sister Natalia, have only exacerbated the stigma by alluring mortals and turning them.

I decided to take a nightly stroll into town. We were weaker in the sun. It gave us pain and made our vision blurry. Some of us were able to withstand its rays, while fledglings were still very vulnerable.

Natalia soon joined me along with a thrall that she acquired. Seeing that there were no bite marks on the tiger, she most likely used mind control on him. The thrall looked at me and gave a menacing growl.

"Calm, Matei," she said as she raised her hand at him. He stood down and nodded at Natalia.

"Yes, my lady," he replied as he bowed.

"A new friend, sister?" I asked with a chuckle. "These, what you call *companions* of yours—you have to see how disturbing this is." I crossed my arms and shook my head. "They can't even control themselves. How can you take pleasure from that?"

"Oh, Stan. Sweet, stupid Stan," she said as she patted my cheek, then slapped it softly. "This is why we have these powers. Why not use them?" She kissed the tiger's cheek and chuckled. "Matei, go home. I shall meet you." He nodded and left for the mansion.

"We need to stop this, Natalia," I said.

"What's wrong about it?" she put her hands on her hips. "If father heard you say that, you would get such a lashing."

"I just don't think we should abuse our powers like this. You are a vampire, not a succubus, Natalia." I shook my head and leaned against a wall. "We drink because we need to. Now it's…it's just sport to you."

"I'm feeling a bit thirsty." She smiled and licked her lips. She then turned around, spread her translucent wings and flew upward. I chuckled; she never listened to anything I said.

Even though she looked like a young adult, like me, Natalia was older—much older than I. Once a vampire becomes such, they stop aging. I stopped counting my own age after 50 or 60 years.

I continued to roam the streets of Bucharest with a hood on my head. I got some looks from passersby, but what would one expect, walking around at night and wearing a mysterious hood? I simply gave them a nod and went about my business. Occasionally, I saw vampires besides Natalia roaming the towns. However, since Bucharest is large, it's a rare but enjoyable occasion to see them stroll casually without fear or hate.

I went to the chapel south of the city. Candles were lit on an altar. I saw my older brother Dorian there as well. His brown, translucent wings flapped slowly, making a breeze against the candles. He secretly prayed to God. I kneeled next to him, folded my hands, and prayed with him.

"Tatăl nostru Care ești în ceruri, sfințească-se numele Tău…" he whispered. *Our Father who art in Heaven, hallowed by Thy name.* "Lead us not into temptation…" he continued. "…and forgive our families harmed by Sanguaris. Provide haven for those harmed by the family. In Your name, we pray."

"Amen," I concluded.

"Even though it seems futile—he may not hear us," Dorian said as he looked at me, "I would like to think we have a sliver of hope, of salvation for you and all of us that leave this world." He smiled at me and I nodded, smiling warmly in return.

"I hope so, too, Dorian. I hope this stigma goes away, or is at least lessened."

Though I decided to leave the chapel, Dorian wished to stay. I waved goodbye to him. Many of the vampires have lost their beliefs; few like Dorian and I remained faithful to the Lord.

As I moved through the town, torches lit the way. I could smell bread baking in one of the houses. At times, a vampire's sense of smell fixated on an individual's blood. A fledgling would quickly pounce at the opportunity. Older vampires are more able to control their cravings.

While walking, down the road, a little lizard boy stopped me. His blood had a familiar scent, as of someone I fed upon years earlier. I scooted past him and continued my journey. I looked back as he continued staring. He soon walked the other way.

Despite my intentions, I found myself following the scent of the boy. Children normally had a strong blood scent. Since they were young, their blood flowed more quickly than adults.

I took to the rooftops and followed the child. As a bat, my vision was better at night, so it was more convenient to sneak around.

Of course I knew it was wrong to stalk and follow a young boy, but... I was just curious. I meant him no harm; I had no intention of drinking. I was just...curious. Could he have been related to someone I'd fed upon before?

I made my way to his house. It was the same house in which I met my first victim decades earlier. I was sure she was still in the house. I circled around it. Some of the outside had been redecorated. Slipping inside, I saw that the shelf of dolls was replaced with a toy shield rack, with accompanying swords. Perhaps for an aspiring fighter? As I continued looking, I saw the victim, fully grown now. There she was, sleeping in her room with a man I assumed was her husband.

I made my way to the boy's room, seeing him smiling as he slept. As I crept back to the entrance, I accidentally knocked over a pot. I gasped, and scrambled to put it back without being noticed. I turned around, startled to see the boy standing in front of me. He gave me an innocent smile and a wave. My head darted from left to right, and I quietly shushed him.

"Hello," he said with a friendly tone. His big, adorable green eyes peered up at mine. His head occasionally tilted from side to side, like a curious puppy. "What were you doing outside our house?"

"Oh I… I was…" I looked around and noticed a few silver coins on the ground. "I lost some of my coins." I picked them up and put them in my pocket. "And now that I've returned them, I must be going. My apologies for waking you." I gave a polite bow and walked away.

The boy stood in front of me, blocked my path, and inspected me. I raised an eyebrow at his curiosity. I squatted and chuckled, meeting him at eye level. "It's rude to stare to stare."

"Why do you have your hood up like that?" He tugged at my hood.

"I'd rather not say," I replied as I straightened my hood.

"Why not? You sound like a nice man."

"Thank you. You're quite the questioning one for someone so young." I chuckled and sighed. "If you insist, but beware." I slowly removed my hood and showed my bat face.

"You're a bat?" he asked as he gasped, but he showed no sign of fear. I nodded and looked away. "Can you fly? Why are your eyes red? Are there any other bats? Can they fly?" His bombardment of questions surprised me, as I thought he would run away or cower.

"How about this, boy: I'll meet you in the market tomorrow, okay? I need to get home, and I'm sure you need your sleep." I smiled as he nodded. "We can talk, and you can ask me anything."

"Do you promise, sir?"

"I promise. I'm Stanislav, but everyone calls me Stan." I extended my hand.

"I am Virgil!" He held my hand and nodded. "I will see you then, Mr. Stan." He hurried back inside and went to bed as I flew away.

The next day, I waited on a rooftop with my hood up to avoid direct contact with the sun. I saw Virgil enter the marketplace. I climbed down and walked into the market.

"There you are!" he said as he jumped up and down. "Were you up on that roof?" I nodded and smiled. "Can I go up there with you?"

"I suppose you can. It might be better that I'm not seen carrying a young boy off." I chuckled and led him to a secluded alley. "People might assume the worst."

I placed the boy on my back and climbed onto the roof. He looked around, his eyes opened wide. The whole city could be seen from here. He sat on the edge and looked up at me with a grin.

"It looks amazing," he said. "It looks like one of my mother's paintings."

"I'm glad you like it, Virgil." I sat down next to him.

He asked me questions about what being a bat was like. Almost every question started with, "My mother told me…" However, he didn't seem to bear any grudge or negative feelings toward me. Then again, he was still just a child. We talked for two more days. It was nice to have a companion to talk to that didn't ramble on about blood and drinking.

We continued a few days after, meeting at the same spot. Did he know about vampires? He never mentioned them during any of our talks. Either way, I did not tell him about it. I already poisoned one child with the knowledge of vampirism; I wasn't ready to poison another. The more we talked, the more worried I became. I couldn't keep up the charade for much longer.

The next week, I decided to end things.

"Virgil, I need to talk to you," I said as I sat down and looked at the lake instead of the town.

"Are you okay, Mr. Stan?" He sat next to me. "You look…troubled. Mr. Stan?" He never let go of the "Mr." from my name. Maybe out of respect.

"We… shouldn't see each other like this anymore." I looked at him then looked away. "It's too dangerous. I think citizens are getting suspicious."

"What do you mean? Are we not friends?"

"Of course we are, but..." I put my hands on the boy's shoulders. "I'm sorry, Virgil." I picked him up and glided back down to the ground. "Go home. Forget everything about me." When he looked away, I put a hand over his head, sending blue energy into him. A soft, low-pitched hum made my ears twitch.

"Did you hear that, Mr. Stan?" he asked as he looked up at me. "What was that?"

It didn't work? I scratched his head. "Oh, uh... here." I took off my necklace. It had a gold pendant with an avian insignia on the back. "For you. So you will have something to remember me by, okay?" I saw a tear roll down his face. "Hey now." I wiped his face and caressed his cheek. "No tears. It'll be okay, Virgil." I gave him a consoling smile.

"Will we ever see each other again? You're the only friend I've ever had, Mr. Stan." Hearing him say that made me sigh. I did want to be his friend, but I didn't want to risk his safety.

"I promise you, we'll meet again someday, Virgil." An empty promise, I was sure. I had hope, though. "I must admit, I do enjoy your company." I chuckled and smiled at the little lizard. This put a big grin on his face, and he then hugged me. I gave him a soft hug in return, inhaling the scent of his blood. "Go on home now, child. We *will* meet again. You have my word." He left the alleyway and disappeared into the crowd. How he wasn't able to see that I was a vampire was baffling. I didn't complain, however. I did as I promised and met him on occasion.

The sun was near setting when I met with the boy. I once again climbed up to the roof with Virgil on my back.

"I have enjoyed these times with you, Virgil." I sat down, looking out at the lake again. The sun reflected its orange rays on the rippling water.

"I agree," he replied as he rubbed his scaly cheek against my arm. "It's nice to have a friend like you, Mr. Stan."

I wrapped a wing around him, almost encasing him fully inside it. He wrapped his arms around me and rested against my side. It felt refreshing to be with someone who wasn't from the mansion or trying to kill me. I felt a warmness spreading through my chest. I was tempted to lick his neck, but resisted the urge. I took a deep breath and inhaled the strong succulent scent. *No, you can do this Stan. He is a sweet boy and doesn't deserve that.* I nuzzled at the boy's head and closed my eyes.

Just as we began to grow closer, the encounters became less frequent. I either saw him with his parents or not at all. As we climbed onto the roof, he wore a look that was less than joyful. His eyes turned toward the town. I caressed his chin and gave a consoling smile.

"My father is getting upset," he said. "I'm in the town too late at night, they say." He looked down and shook his head. "I really don't like this at all, but…"

"I see," I replied as I sighed quietly. "Does this mean…?"

He nodded, and sighed. "I wanted to give you this before you left." He handed me a doll made of straw. "I've been making this for a week. I want you to have it." It looked almost like me without the wings. The red buttons for eyes and the little straw ears made me smile. He even gave it a hood and cloak like what I wore. On the back of the cloak, there was an insignia like on the pendant I gave him.

"Virgil, this is…nobody has ever given me a gift like this before. I will always cherish it." I kissed the doll and held it close.

"Virgil?" A man called out. "Virgil! Where are you, son?"

"One day we'll meet again, Mr. Stan. I promise." Virgil kissed my hand and nodded. I flew down with him and let him on the ground.

"Take care of yourself, boy." I put my hands on his shoulders. "You'll be in my thoughts."

"And you in mine," he replied. I heard his parents shouting for him. As he left, he turned around and waved to me. I returned the wave with a weaker one of my own, and a smile. Maybe this was for the best?

Days go by, then months, then years. My mind becomes occupied with the rise of a group that hunts vampires: Salvatori de Solare—Saviors of the Sun. They are a holy group of warriors and clerics who aim to destroy any kind of "beasts against God" as they call them, which includes vampires. We've had a few encounters with them.

We lost our father in a skirmish at our home. Natalia took charge of the family. Her one goal was to wipe out the Salvatori. While I agreed with her goal to an extent, her rule in the family drove wedges between me and other members. *No matter what*, she said, *no matter who gets in our way, we will crush the Salvatori*.

One day she slammed open the door to my room as I sat on my bed. "What have I told you?" she shouted. "Stop going out during the day! Lest you get caught by the hunters and they stake and burn you. Is that what you want, boy?" She crossed her arms and glared at me.

"I've done no harm!" I argued. "You are putting innocents in danger with this campaign of yours. Stop trying to act like father. You bring men here for your disposal. You're nothing but a glorified whore!"

"You will not speak to me in that way." She smacked me, her claws barely making marks on my cheek. Her eyes calmed as she sighed. "Father is gone, and this family needed someone to lead them—guide them. I stood forward when nobody else would. I am the matriarch of blood, boy. Unless…you wish to step forward?"

I looked away. She knew I had no interest in leading the family. She was also much stronger than me. However… calling herself the matriarch of blood as if she were the first-made vampire put a lump in my stomach.

"I thought so," she said with a scoff. "Weak, boy. Very weak." She headed for the door as I looked at her.

"You've changed, Natalia," I said.

She stopped and giggled, still facing away from me. "For the better, dear Stan," she replied. "For the better."

She left me alone, and I caught a glance at the doll. I took it off the table next to my bed and held it to my chest. "A matriarch, she calls it." I looked at the doll's red buttons. "What have you been doing all this time? I hope you're safe."

At times, Natalia ordered vampires to scout at night for Salvatori. Almost all the citizens cowered into their homes. Others would decorate their homes with crosses, candles, and the like to ward off vampires. Despite this, some vampires would kill straggling citizens in the streets for being witnesses. On Natalia's order, and much to our resentment, Dorian, I, and three other vampires headed into one of the Salvatori's encampments outside of town. A raven flew down and landed on Dorian's hand. He kissed its head and sent it away. That meant the area was unguarded. I heard him give a soft but frustrated sigh. I looked at him, but he kept his eyes on the encampment.

"Rămâi tăcut," Dorian whispered as he motioned forward. *Stay silent.*

We scouted the area and saw that everyone was asleep, a fire glowing in the middle of the camp. My eyes were drawn to one member who was sleeping on his back in one of the tents. Seeing a long green tail, I realized that it was a lizard, and he was wearing the same necklace that I gave Virgil. It *was* him! I never thought I'd see him again!

"Virgil?" I whispered as I came closer. "Virgil." I gave him a soft tap and a nudge. He slowly woke up and opened his eyes.

"S-Stan?" he asked with a weak voice as he rubbed his eyes. His voice was lower and he looked like a full adult lizard now, even stubbly above his lip and around his face. He leaped up and gave me a hug. His stubble tickled as he rubbed his face against mine. "What are you doing here? You shouldn't be here." He looked around.

"What am I doing here? What are you?" I noticed that the necklace also had a cross on the end of it. "What…what is this?" I touched it but flinched at the sting of it. He took me away from the encampment.

"I'm with the Salvatori, now." He looked at my hand and saw a little singe. "Why did that hurt you, Stan? Are you a…"

"I suppose there's no use hiding it, anymore." I held Virgil's hands. "Yes, I am a vampire." I kissed his hands. "Please don't think differently of me. I'm still Stan. I'm still the same bat you met as a child." I saw a slight scowl on his face as he looked away. "You're mad."

"I'm not mad, just…disappointed." He sighed. "We're friends, Stan. I thought you could trust me with anything. You lied to me. You've been lying all this time. The only thing that mattered to me was that you were my friend—vampire or not. My father taught me that not all bats were vampires, and not all vampires were bats. Even so, I was just happy to have you as a friend."

"I do trust you, Virgil." I put my hand on his chest. "I didn't want you to get involved in all…this."

"I joined the Salvatori on my own. My mother killed herself because of vampirism. She suffered what my father called Sanguaris. The only way you could get it, he said, is by the bite of a vampire." He put his head on my chest and shed tears. I held him close. "A wretched disease, he called it. Wretched enough to kill her."

I let go of him and shook my head. "Virgil," I said with a sigh. "It was me. I gave her the disease," I said as he let go of me.

"What?" he looked up at me as his eyes twinkled with tears.

"It was decades ago." I walked away into a darkened area of the town as he followed. "I was out on my first night of drinking, and I smelled the sweetest blood. It felt like her blood was calling and—anyway, she was a little girl and…I'm sorry, Virgil." I turned to him and held his hands. "Truly, I'm so sorry."

He looked away and hesitated. "Stan," he said as he looked at me. "You're a vampire. There are citizens and the Salvatori that won't hesitate to hunt you down." He caressed my cheek. "I…I want to kill you right now, but…" He sat down and sighed. "I just can't. I thought we could have had something. I cared for you; I maybe even…"

"Virgil," I said as I caressed his cheek as well. I held him close to me. I exhaled as I felt our cold embrace. I felt his warm heart beat against my chest. He soon broke from the hug and turned away from me.

"The only reason I'm letting you live now is because of what we had years ago." He held my hands again and gave a disgruntled sigh. "The Salvatori are where I belong now. They took me in—called me their family. To let them down would be…"

"I understand, Virgil," I replied. "If it were any different…"

"Well, everything happens for a reason." He shook his head. "My mother always told me that." As I tried to hold his hand, he snatched it away. "Go, Stan. Please go. I don't want to see you hurt. But if we do cross paths again, I swear, if we cross again, Stan…"

"You know, Virgil? I'd welcome it. If it must be done by anyone, I would be glad it's you." I began to walk away. I looked back at him. "Maybe this is what God intended?"

"Maybe so. If it is, may He have mercy on both of us. Goodbye, Stan." He nodded and crossed himself. I flew away, abandoning the other vampires at the camp.

I flew to the outskirts of the Wallachian Plains. I found a small, abandoned shack for refuge. After a month, I was able to settle in and call the cleaned-up hovel my new home.

I went back into town at night with my hood down. It was nearly abandoned. I saw bats hovering over buildings. Natalia's authority must have gotten out of control. The sky had a weak red hue to it, as if Satan himself had painted it. I saw some vampires fighting Salvatori members. The hunters were using crossbows, most likely to keep the bats at bay. They wore wooden stakes on belts around their waists.

I smelled garlic coming toward me as I saw citizens flee. Garlic didn't have any negative effects on us, although our noses were extra-sensitive to the scent.

"Bloodsucker! Bloodsucker!" one of the women cried out as she ran away holding up her garlic.

"Bloodsucker?" I repeated with a chuckle. "I have never *sucked* blood before. I drink it."

Another citizen threw a vial of liquid at me. It only hit my arm and burned like the morning sun. That must have been the holy water that the chapels used. He chanted "The power of Christ compels you! The power of Christ compels you!"

I knocked the vial out of his hand and flew away. Something pierced one of my wings; a crossbow bolt. I slammed into a building and hit the ground. Two of the Salvatori surrounded me on either side. I then heard Dorian give a roaring cry as he swooped down to tackle one of the Salvatori. Surprised, the other one took a desperate shot but missed. I rushed to him and bit him on the neck, then ripped his flesh apart with my fangs.

"Stan, you're alive?" Dorian asked as he hugged me. "We searched for you, but Natalia forced us to stop. She thought you were holding her back. You're better to us dead and out of the way, she said."

"She…she said that?" I gave a soft groan as I shook my head. "I knew that power was consuming her, but to cast her brother aside… I'm worried for her and the family. What is stopping her from turning others? We need to stop her, Dorian." I put my hands on his shoulders. "This whole war between the two factions…it's costing innocent lives. I know you might disagree, but-"

"No, she is taking this issue into her own hands for selfish gain," he said, crossing his arms. "She wants power. She's gone mad with it."

"It's good that we all agree then," said a familiar voice. I looked around to see a lizard emerge from the alleyway along with three Salvatori. The hunters had their bows aimed at us.

"You," I said softly. I looked at Dorian as he looked back at me with his head tilted.

"You know this one, Stan?" he asked.

I nodded and took a step toward Virgil. A cock of the crossbow stopped me in my tracks.

"On your order, captain," one of the members said to Virgil as they readied their crossbows.

Virgil held his hand up. "No." He looked sternly at me. "Leave us." The members looked at each other and lowered their weapons.

"But…" another argued, "captain—"

"Leave us," he repeated with a raised voice. "Now!" They scurried off, dropping a few bolts behind them in their haste.

"Captain, is it?" I asked as crossed my arms.

"I rose through the ranks," he replied as he crossed his own arms. "I took the oath, and now…I'm a captain of the Salvatori. Beside the point; I heard what you two were talking about."

"Who are you, boy?" Dorian interjected. "Just another vampire hunter?"

"He's my—was my friend, Dorian," I replied. He crossed his arms and looked at Virgil. "Do not worry." I turned toward the lizard. "What do you want? Surely not to reconcile?"

"I want the same thing as you do," Virgil replied as he looked up to the soaring bats. "We need to stop this Natalia. She is destroying this city."

"It seems worse than we thought," said Dorian as he saw more Salvatori and vampires clashing. "She has trained her mind powers, making herself powerful. Many of my brothers have attacked me; many of them I know wouldn't have dared to attack anyone *for the family* as they so put it."

"We have been trying to make our way to the mansion, but we got sidetracked with…this." Virgil motioned to the dead bats, Salvatori, and citizens alike sprawled across the blood-splattered streets.

"We can take you there," I said. "If we work together, we can end this, Virgil." The lizard nodded and I looked to Dorian.

"I'm not too eager to work with these Salvatori." Dorian shook his head and looked at me. "However, I'm less eager to see Natalia spread her rule over Romania. We should go to the mansion. I'll take the lead." He flew off and left us behind.

We stood there for a moment in awkward silence. Virgil then pulled out the necklace I gave him. "I never went anywhere without this," he said.

I showed him the doll tied to my belt and smiled softly. He held my hand and rubbed it against his cheek.

"What do you think will happen after this is over?" I asked. "To us, I mean? Do you think we could…salvage any of this?"

"Perhaps," he replied. Hearing that made me smile. "I'll admit I have missed you after our…encounter. Wondering if you were okay, wondering if…you were thinking about me." He blushed and looked away.

"I was," I replied as I turned his head to face me. "Every time I saw the doll, you came into my mind."

"Let's finish this together, Stan." He nodded at me and kissed my hand. I swept him off his feet and flew off with him in my arms.

When we made our way to the mansion, I saw vampires and Salvatori fighting. One vampire grabbed a Salvatori member and flew high into the sky, then let go of the man;, his scream could be heard as he fell to his doom. As we landed, we fought through both Salvatori and vampires. I searched for Dorian. I didn't see him in the courtyard, so we headed inside.

Vampires were fighting the Salvatori here too. It was a bloodbath. In the midst of all this, I saw Dorian on the upper level. I flew upstairs as Virgil followed close behind, but, we were too late to save him. One Salvatori jumped on Dorian's back and staked him in the heart. He let out a painful groan, coughing blood as he fell to the floor.

"Dorian, no!" I shouted as I ran over to him, intending to help him up…

"No," the bat replied with another cough. "No, Stan. It's too late for me. Centuries of this cursed disease has come to an end for me. Kill…Natalia." He pulled the wooden stake out of his own heart and gave it to me. "Pierce... her twisted… heart." He took one final gasp as his head slumped backward.

"Rest in peace, brother," I said as I closed his eyes. I stood up and looked at Virgil. He held out his hand and crossed Dorian. "We need to get to Natalia."

We rushed to father's old room, which Natalia had made her own. She was in the big room, sitting in his chair, legs crossed, wearing his cloak as if she was father now.

"Stop this, Natalia," I said as I stepped forward. "You've gone too far! Dorian is dead."

"Another obstacle set aside, then," she replied as she flicked her dark brown hair. "Though, I must admit I am surprised you're still alive. Stronger than I thought. You have my praise."

"I don't want your praise," I replied as I scowled at her. "I want you to stop this!"

Her eyes glowed a bright orange. I heard Virgil grunt as he held his head. "S-stan..." he pleaded. "Stop her." His eyes shone a dim orange as he pulled out a wooden stake from his belt and rushed toward me.

"What are you doing?" I asked as I dodged his attacks. He continued aiming for my heart, but I grabbed his arms.

"It's...it's not me, Stan!" He almost struck my chest with his next swing! I grabbed his arms and held the stake away from me.

"Yes, Yes!" Natalia shouted. "Kill each other! Kill him Virgil!"

"K-kill me," he cried out. "Kill me, Stan!"

"What? No!" I looked at him, shocked at his words. "I'm not going to kill you, Virgil."

"If you don't...I'll kill you!" I saw tears sliding down his cheeks as we struggled. Tears fell from my eyes as well. "Do it...Stan." I looked into his eyes as they grew brighter, hearing him grunt and aiming at my chest.

I shook my head and let out a slight sob.

"Do it, Stan!" he shouted. "Hurry! I can't...control..."

As he groaned in pain, he escaped my grip and attempted the stab. Moving out of the way, I sank my fangs into his neck. This broke the control that Natalia had over him. He gasped from the bite as his eyes returned to normal. He fell to a knee and looked at me.

"Stan?" He blinked as he looked up to me, caressing my cheek.

"It's me, Virgil. I am here." I smiled at him, putting my hand on his shoulder.

"No, no, no!" Natalia cried out as she stomped on the floor. "You weren't supposed to bite him, you idiot!"

I heard her growl, then scream. As she dashed at us with a wooden stake of her own, Virgil opened his eyes wide and stood in front of me, and grabbed her hand in attempt to stop her. However, she overpowered him and pierced his chest deeply. As she pulled the stake out, Virgil fell into my arms.

As I held Virgil, he managed to utter one last sentence, "I...love...you...Stan."

"I... I love you too...Virgil." I sobbed and kissed his head. I gently laid him on the floor. My head and heart felt heavy.

"No!" Natalia shouted, "You were supposed to kill each other!"

She unsheathed her claws and growled. I picked up the blood-stained stake as a scorching heat of anger radiated through my body. I looked up and saw her charging at me. I reacted quickly, ducking under Natalia's claws and piercing her heart. She gasped and coughed out blood. "N-no," she said.

I grunted and pushed her against the wall, driving the stake in deeper. "It ends, Natalia." I saw tears in her shocked eyes.

"I can't..." she said weakly. "It can't...end like this." She fell to the ground and grabbed my hand. Her grip rapidly became feeble, and she soon let go.

"Rest in peace, sister." I closed her eyes and stood up.

Looking out to the courtyard of the estate, I saw more Salvatori and fewer vampires. The Salvatori carried torches; perhaps readying to burn the mansion down? They began firing flaming bolts at the vampires. Screams of pain could be heard from the bats struck with torches. Death cries filled the night from those who were staked.

The wooden floors started to burn, flames spreading up the beams and banners on the walls. I wasn't about to let Virgil die here. I picked up my lizard friend and looked for an exit. The hunters began running upstairs toward me. I could barely see the exit downstairs. I spread my wings and flew. I beamed past the Salvatori, knocking some down the steps, my wings burning from their torches, but I endured...for him. I made my way through the open doors and flew away from the mansion.

In the air there was much less fighting. I wasn't sure whether the bats had died or surrendered. I wasn't curious enough to land.

I proceeded to the chapel where Dorian had prayed. After placing Virgil on the floor, I lit candles around the altar. I raised my hand and crossed him, then closed my eyes and put my hands together.

"Sfinte Dumnezeule, Sfinte tare, Sfinte şi de moarte, miluieste-ne pe noi," I prayed. *Holy God, Holy Mighty, Holy and Immortal, have mercy on us.* "Give rest with the Saints to the soul of Your servant where there is neither pain, grief, nor sighing, but life everlasting."

Like my mother said, every beginning must have an ending. Every story must come to an end.

Kamogawa
Sekigahara, Japan - 1600 CE

As I looked out on the foggy battlefield of Sekigahara, I felt a soothing breeze on my face and my three tails. I caught a faint glimpse of the orange sun setting over the horizon. Walking toward the southwestern garrison, there was the strong smell of gunpowder being loaded into the cannons. The moon shone weakly through the fog and clouds. I looked into the reflection of a puddle from the rain earlier today and caught a glimpse of a white feline. Hideki? It couldn't be—he defected to the Ishida army. Perhaps it was just the lack of sleep playing with my eyes. I knew it wasn't right to worry about the enemy, but still…

"Eyes front, Akio," said Tadakatsu as he peered at me with stoic brown eyes. The deer continued forward to Ieyasu's garrison as his officers and I followed behind him. There was no sign of the Ishida army yet.

As we arrived at the garrison, the moon rose high above the fog—no sign of stars yet. I sat and leaned against the weapon rack. Despite trying to focus my mind upon the upcoming battle, I thought about Hideki. After he defected, we discreetly met at night. However, those occurrences became less and less, until he stopped meeting me altogether. *I miss you. I miss…the time we spent, Hide-kun.* I shook my head and looked up to the moon again. He was like a recurring sweet dream—and a nightmare—haunting me at the same time.

My eyes soon started to close. I struggled to keep them open, but my body needed rest. Soon, however, a bellow woke me, making me spring to my feet.

"Akio!" Tadakatsu called as he walked toward me. "You're standing on my pike."

I looked down and noticed I was standing on the blade. "Oh, my apologies, sensei." I stepped back as he raised his unusually large weapon. It was more fitting for someone of his large stature and musculature. I only came up to his chest. His antlers also added to the intimidating visage.

Seeing the coast was clear, I decided to abandon my post and walk into the night. As I moved away from the fog, the moon shone through the trees. Visions of my times with Hideki rushed through my head. *I wish you were here. But now you're the enemy.* Sighing, I brushed my hand along a tree and continued walking.

The buzzing of insects filled the air, along with the occasional hooting owl. The only source of light was the moon gleaming in the forest. I treaded carefully to avoid bumping into or tripping over anything. Soon, I saw the clearing. The grass swaying in the wind made me smile. My ears folded down as my tails swayed with the grass. Just beyond the opening was where it all started—where Hideki and I became closer than ever—Kamogawa.

I remembered us going for a swim in the river when we were cubs. He always teased me about going bare in the water, pulling on my fundoshi and splashing water at me. Once in a while, we saw someone filling a bucket or washing themselves.

As I arrived at the river, the water reflected a milky white from the moon. Fireflies flew above the river. I noticed ripples in the water to the right of me. I turned my head and noticed a familiar feline naked in the river.

"Hide-kun?" I called, as he looked at me and smiled. Without a thought, I ran into the water fully clothed and hugged the cat tightly. "It's so good to see you, Hide-kun! What are you doing here? What if someone sees?" I looked around nervously as he put two fingers on my lips and shushed me.

"It's good to see you too, Aki-kun." He smiled at me and stroked my ears softly.

I began removing my clothing and armor, tossing the pieces in the grass. "What made you come here?"

Hideki chuckled. "The same reason you did, perhaps. Memories? Peace of mind? Hoping that you would show?" He looked at the flowing water. "We need to remain discreet, however. People might realize what we're doing. They might think we were conspiring. I'd rather that not happen to either of us. That's why I came to you less and less. Others were getting suspicious. I'm sorry I couldn't tell you before. I had to keep some things hidden."

"I was worried for you, brother." I looked away. "I thought you forgot about me." I looked at him with a smile, resting my head on his chest. "I'm glad you're here and safe, though."

"You know, Aki-kun, this reminds me of that time when we were young." He sighed in contentment, rubbing my back. "You were always so scared to take off your clothes, as if I was going to attack you." He chuckled.

"As if that stopped you from attacking me anyway?" I splashed at the cat and swam around. "Have you no shame, Hide-kun?" I asked, and shook my head with a chuckle.

"I never had any shame!" He grinned, stood proudly, and crossed his arms, flaunting his sheathed weapon.

"Just like when we were young." I swam toward him and smiled. "You haven't changed a bit, Hideki."

"Neither have you, Aki-kun." He smiled and wrapped his arms around my small waist.

We swam around a while longer. We laughed and talked more. My worries of others went away, though I noticed a look of concern on Hideki's face.

I tilted my head. "Hide-kun?"

"Do you remember those two soldiers we saw upon Arashiyama?" Hideki asked. "How we wanted to mimic them in becoming blood brothers?" Hideki asked as he looked up at the full moon. I nodded. "Even though you were too scared to do it?"

"Hey now, there was no reason to slit our hands," I replied with a chuckle. "Besides, after all these years, us being here proves that we don't need to perform a ritual to show our friendship, Hide-kun." The cat's purring made ripples in the water. I held his hands. "I'm sorry, I..." I let go of his hands. "I don't mean to make you feel uncomfortable or anything." I looked away, embarrassed. "I just..."

"Aki-kun, if I was uncomfortable..." He nuzzled my cheek, and I felt it warm in response. Hopefully he didn't notice my blush. "...would I be with you right now in the river, with nothing but my fur?" Hearing that made me let out a soft, happy murr. "It's not like I haven't thought about..." His face began turning red.

"What, the ritual?" I asked. "You really think that—"

"Not that, Akio." He grabbed my hands. "Us. The times I've spent alone at this river, I've thought about you. I've missed you."

"I feel the same way, Hideki," I replied. "I've always thought of you as...more than a brother."

The cat's ears perked up, and he looked away. I noticed his cheeks turning pink and smiled at him.

"I have too, Akio." He returned the smile and put a hand on my shoulder. "Why do you think I was trying to get you to disrobe all those times?" He giggled and shook his head. "But I digress. I do feel the same way. I want to be more than just friends—brothers." He held my hands. "Once this war is over, Akio, I want you to be my lover."

"But how could we possibly..." I looked away. "You're on the other side, Hide-kun. If I have to face you in battle, I—"

"You won't, Aki-kun. Lord Ieyasu and Hanzō-sensei said something important about the battle." I wasn't sure what he was talking about, but I listened anyway. "There are four people who are key to turning the tide of this battle: Shima Sakon—defeat him, and you'll have control of the southwestern cannons; Ankokuji Ekei—kill him, and you'll surely lower Mitsunari's morale; Kobayakawa Hideaki—some others will deal with him; and Uesugi Kagekatsu—deal with him last. Mitsunari has already lost the Seven Spears."

"Why are you telling me this, Hide-kun?" I asked. He looked at me, eyes filled with concern.

"I want you to live, Aki-kun," he said. "I want you to live." Tears rolled down my face. He held me tight. "After this battle, I want us both to be alive and well." I wrapped my arms around him and returned the hug. "Akio, I want to share something with you." I could hear a faint stutter in his words.

"What is it?" I tilted my head.

"This night," he answered. "I want it to be one to remember," Hideki said in a hushed tone. "Akio," he whispered in my ear, "I want to make love to you."

Hearing this made my eyes open wide. "H-Hideki," I stuttered. "Hideki, I…" At that moment, he planted his muzzle against mine. My face became flushed, and my hands tingled.

I returned the kiss with a soft, shuddering gasp. He slid his tongue into my mouth. I pressed my tongue along his, as my hands made their way to his chest and sculpted stomach.

"You've gotten stronger, I can feel," I said as I smiled up at him, rubbing along his sides.

"And you've gotten fluffier, fox," he replied as he felt along my chest and stomach, and chuckled. "I remember that one time we…explored ourselves here. I don't recall us finishing." He winked.

"Well, we have all night." I rubbed my hands along his back as he purred in response. We climbed out of the river and lay in the soft grass. With sheath against sheath, chest against chest, I couldn't help reaching down to feel his sheath throb against my own. At my touch he let out a deep moan, and his hands slid over my sheath as well..

I held him close, wrapping my legs around his waist. I took in the scent of his arousal. So intoxicating. Soon, we were both hard and throbbing against each other.

I thrust against him and moaned softly. I enjoyed feeling the barbs on Hideki's member, the sensation arousing me more. He returned the favor, panting in my ear as he nibbled on it. I began panting as my tongue lolled out.

My member continued to pulse against his as he let go of my ear and kissed me again. I kissed him deeper as he thrust against me. "Hide-kun," I said hesitantly. I looked away and blushed, then looked back at him. I felt my muscles tighten, and my heart pounded faster.

He put his hand on my chest to feel it racing. "Relax, Akio. Trust me." He laid me on my back. I nodded and smiled, relaxing my nerves. He kissed me again, my body almost going limp from the pleasure of the simple touch of his muzzle.

He leaned down and licked at my member, causing my knot to emerge. I felt pre leaking onto my stomach as my member throbbed even harder. Hideki licked my tip to catch each drop. The feeling was so pleasurable that my body couldn't help shuddering with pure lust.

After pulling him off my cock and pressing my muzzle against his, I slid my tongue into his maw, pressing against his own tongue. He slid a finger into my entrance, making me gasp and moan against his muzzle. I felt his body trembling as our fur brushed together. I wrapped my arms around his muscular back as he started to thrust his member against mine again. His pre made his member slick against mine, making him slide and thrust quicker against me.

Suddenly Hideki stopped moving and eased his finger from my passage, then lifted my legs, pushing his cock into my tight hole. I moaned out, hugging him tight as he began moving inside me. He groaned and buried his face in my neck fur.

I could feel a warm sensation inside me waiting to explode. The sounds of Hideki's panting against my neck, the lingering taste of his muzzle against mine, and the smell of sweet lust filling the air was enough to drive anyone feral. The more his cock hit my sensitive spot, the more I lost control, growling and whining. His purring above me only intensified my pleasure.

Soon enough, he started groaning, then bit my shoulder with his sharp fangs. Though he drew a bit of blood, I was too in the moment to care. I felt the passion build inside me, then overwhelm me as I released my seed all over our bodies, letting out a loud moan as I orgasmed. At that moment, he let out bursts of his own seed deep inside me. He panted and collapsed on top of me as I groaned against his neck, rubbing the back of his head.

"Akio," he said, trying to catch his breath, "I love you." As I heard that, I felt a warmness in my heart and stomach. My face was flaming hot and red.

"I love you too, Hideki. I...want this to last," I told him. I took a deep sigh and looked him in the eyes. "I want to be with you. I want to spend my life with you, Hideki. I..." I hesitated, "I love you, Hideki. I love you." I held him tight, pressing my muzzle to his neck.

"Then I promise, I'll make it back to you, Aki-kun." He smiled at me, resting his forehead against mine. "I'll soon be by your side in battle; I'll protect you." Part of me didn't understand what he meant, but his words still comforted me.

The next morning, Hideki was gone. I saw a note next to a sword by the side of the river. *We will make it through this, Aki-kun,* it read. *I'll see you on the battlefield.*

I hurried my way to Sekigahara, barely able to put my armor on. The battle had already begun amidst the fog. I heard the warriors' battle cries and the swords clanging and clashing. As I moved around the battlefield, I heard cannon fire coming from the south garrison.

Sakon... I began holding my own against the enemy. *Ekei. Kobayakawa—don't worry about him and Kagekatsu.* I headed toward the cannons being controlled by Sakon. I was, however, intercepted by Hideki.

"Wh-what are you doing here?" I yelled above the cannon fire.

"You'll see," he replied. "Defeat Sakon. Then go after Ekei." He nodded at me and left.

I headed toward Sakon's garrison, where officers were already fighting. With their aid, I defeated his cannoneers, and then slew Sakon. I continued to Ekei's garrison. He was already under attack by archers! But who led the attack? Arrows were flying past the old owl.

"Keep firing, men!" It was Hideki! Had he been feigning allegiance this whole time? I ran up to the cat.

"Hideki!" I called out. He simply smiled at me and resumed shooting with his own bow. Eventually the owl plummeted to the ground. Ekei was slain! "You… you really are on our side?" I asked with an ecstatic smile. He nodded with a smile of his own. I hugged him tight. "You'll soon be by my side. That's what you meant."

"And I always will be." He kissed my forehead. "Come, Aki-kun, we have a battle to win. For Lord Ieyasu!" The men cheered at his words.

We readied our blades and charged into battle together. With the cannons stopped and the plan going our way, we continued. Kagekatsu was slain, and Kobayakawa defected. The fog soon lifted as well. Victory was assured!

Hideki kept his word. He stayed by my side, and I never left his. I had his back, and he had mine. We fought as one. The battle was nearing an end as we cut down the enemy. We made our way to the Ishida main camp where we saw Ieyasu execute Mitsunari. The enemy commander fell to the ground, a spear plunged through his back.

The battle was over. The Tokugawa army was victorious. A new age was upon us. Japan was once again unified under the Tokugawa banner!

Once we started celebrating, Hideki swept me away from the bloodstained battlefield. My hand in his, he took me back to Kamogawa. The sun was nearly set by the time we arrived.

"It's beautiful, isn't it?" he asked, sitting at the edge of the river. I sat next to him and rested my head on his shoulder.

"It is. Even better when I get to spend these moments with you." I looked up at him and gave a soft murr. "What do we do now?"

"Well…we won." Hideki replied as he held me close. "Usually a victory is celebrated." I nodded and chuckled.

"Should we go back to the other men?"

"And miss a moment of this? Never." Hideki pressed his lips against mine, wrapping his arms around my waist. "No matter what happens, Aki-kun, whatever we go through, whatever comes our way in the future, I'll be by your side."

"Hide-kun." I held him tightly, resting my head on his chest.

"This feels...it feels like a dream." I looked into his sapphire eyes. "It feels much stronger than a blood oath, Hide-kun."

"It feels like our bond is inseparable. I'm glad, though. I wouldn't want it any other way. I love you, Akio."

"I love you too, Hideki."

From that day forward, we continued our lives as one.

ᘓhe Beast
Massachusetts, Colonial America - 1654 CE

Another fox stood at the gallows before a crowd of citizens. She was barely an adult. Beneath the overcast of clouds and the slight rainfall, someone cried. The fox girl's mother held onto her husband as they watched from the crowd. "Evil woman!" some shouted.

"Susan Welsh!" bellowed the German Shepherd Reverend Williams. "You have been accused of witchcraft! What have you to say in your defense?"

"I've done nothing to Harold's inn!" she pleaded. "I beg of you, Reverend, please let me free!"

"Liar!" Harold replied. "I saw the glasses moving. She was standing outside my inn as I felt a pressure on me! It was as if I was being pushed and pulled! It must've been her. Nobody else was around."

"I was just waiting for my mother!" she replied. "Mother, please! You know I wouldn't do anything like this!"

"I don't know what to believe anymore, Susan," her mother replied, sobbing softly.

Susan gasped, her eyes widening and ears twitching. A hooded bear tied her hands with rope. With the hangman's noose in hand, he wrapped it around her neck. Tears fell from her face onto the wooden platform. With the fox ready to be hung, the bear walked over to the lever and looked at Reverend Williams. As the German Shepherd nodded, the bear pulled the lever. In that instant, the floor below her opened up, and she was hung by her neck.

While some looked at the warm corpse as if justice had been served; others, like me, my friend Thomas, and Susan's family looked on in despair. Thomas and I left the crowd and headed home. As we walked, Thomas folded his ears down.

"Thomas?" I looked at him concerned, my ears folded as well.

"That poor girl," he replied, shaking his head. "Her family. The way her mother looked at her as if any love for her had disappeared."

"I know," I replied with a sigh. "The second family torn apart by this witchcraft nonsense."

"Perhaps it is just nonsense." He had an inquisitive look on his face. "Then again…"

"What was that?"

"Oh, nothing; just thinking aloud."

As we returned to our little hovel, the clouds and rain went away. I heard howling of the feral wolves in the forest as Thomas' ears perked up. He sat at the kitchen table and gave a sigh as he looked out the window. He took his shoes off and rubbed his feet. I started fixing dinner and washing dishes.

Thomas worked at the lumber mill just outside of town. He had been there for 15 years. He'd grown stronger from the work since I'd last seen him.

He sighed and looked at me, his head rested on his hand. "You don't believe she was guilty; do you, Ed?"

"I'm not sure," I replied. I tried to stay clear of any superstitious nonsense that people came up with. Being a black cat, however, I'd come into my own bad luck, and many people stayed clear of me. There were a few instances with collapsing ladders, chairs breaking, and even a couple of burnt dinners. Why Thomas decided to live with me still baffled me, but I didn't complain.

"It's almost as bad as the lycan drivel that's been spreading." He leaned back in his chair and crossed his arms. "Harold was always a sneaky porker. Never liked the bastard."

"Plenty of…interesting things have happened ever since she moved to Salem though," I replied as I rubbed the back of my head. "You can't deny the unusual occurrences." I finished cooking and gave Thomas his dinner.

"I suppose you're right, but witches?" He began to eat. "It's a bit over the top. Also weren't werewolf trials in Europe?"

"That's what I've been told, but who knows?" I said. "One of the other wolves fell victim last week to a supposed witch attack. He was foaming at the mouth and looked bigger than usual." I raised an eyebrow at him. "For all we know, you could be a lycan. You have been getting bigger." I laughed and poked his belly.

"Hey now," he said with a chuckle. "Nobody has complained about it before."

"Nor am I complaining now," I replied as I gave his belly a soft rub.

After I finished cleaning the dishes, I sat down and ate as well. Thomas got up and cleaned his dishes

"I think I'll go to bed early," Thomas said as he put his plate away. "I really hope that I don't turn into one of those beasts overnight." He chuckled. "That would rip and tear my clothes."

"Wouldn't want that now, would we?" I replied with a giggle. He smiled and headed to bed. I got up and walked over to the window. I saw the moon shining brightly, not a star in sight. As beautiful as it was, it didn't really take my mind off of these suspicions.

I soon slumped into the bed next to Thomas'. Even though we were in separate beds, I had a smile on my face knowing that we were sleeping together. I exhaled softly and drifted off to sleep.

When I woke up the next morning, I found a note on the table:

I'll be at the mill for most of the day. I made you breakfast and laid out your work boots for the fields. Until tonight, Ed. Take care.

Thomas

On that note, I changed into my work clothes, then went into the kitchen and ate my breakfast. I sighed, my ears flat as I looked at the empty wooden chair in front of me. Perhaps it was quiet. Perhaps I wished he was here with me. Perhaps I was bored.

I went into the kitchen and cleaned my plate, then put on my boots and went into the fields. While the feral wolves' howls would soothe Thomas, the sound ruffled my fur. We'd had issues with feral animals running amok in the fields, eating the harvest. I took my pitchfork just in case any lurked in the fields.

As I was harvesting wheat in the fields, I saw Reverend Williams walking toward me.

"Edmund!" he called as he waved and approached.

"Hello there, Reverend." I waved back to the dog. "How can I help you today?"

"Have you heard about the incident with Miss Eileen?"

I shook my head as I leaned on my pitchfork. "What happened? Is she okay?"

"She claimed that she couldn't breathe. She gasped as if being choked." He crossed his arms.

"Oh dear."

"When her little servant girl Abigail showed, her husband Lawrence quickly accused her of being a witch. Eileen is resting now."

"Could it be a coincidence? Perhaps she took ill?" I raised an eyebrow.

"Mysterious times, indeed," said the reverend. "First little Susan, now Abigail."

"Do you think Susan was behind the incident at Harold's inn?" I asked. "You don't believe in this witch commotion, do you, Reverend?"

"I don't know, son. But whatever is going on, we need to find out soon." He shook his head and sighed. "The whole town is becoming hysterical. You'd probably know best about superstition, eh?" He looked at me head-to-toe and laughed. The laughter trailed off, though, and he put his hand on my shoulder. "There's…also been some unrest at the mill, Edmund. Tell Thomas to be careful."

"I will," I replied with a nod. "Thank you, Reverend."

"The Lord be with you." He crossed me and nodded.

"And with you, Reverend." I replied as he walked away.

Knowing that Thomas might be in danger, I headed to the mill. I didn't want him to get hurt. As I walked through the fields, I heard more wolves howling. I shuddered and paced faster. *You beasts are very chatty today*, I thought. They must have missed Thomas.

I made my way to the mill. It reeked of burning wood and foul odors from the strong working men. I looked around for the wolf.

"Excuse me," I called out to a worker, walking up to him. "Have you seen Thomas anywhere? Thomas Summers?"

"He's probably getting some logs from behind the mill," he replied, pointing toward the back of the building. I went back outside and looked around.

"Thomas?" I called, seeing the big wolf carrying a log with ease as two other workers struggled to carry one. "Well, there you are."

"Oh!" he dropped his log. The two men behind him tripped over it and dropped their own as well. "Sorry," he said as he helped them pick it back up and put his log to the side of the mill. "To what do I owe this visit?"

"How is work? Nothing out of the ordinary?" I looked around the mill, seeing everyone working and the saw cutting the logs normally. "Nothing strange?"

"Everything is fine, Ed. Calm down," he replied as he ruffled my head fur. "What brought this on, hmm?"

"Reverend said there was some unrest here," I said with a chuckle. "Not sure why he thought of that." I scratched my ear and shrugged.

"Williams is quite the paranoid one sometimes. Maybe he came here at night, causing a commotion and trying to start a ruckus." He shrugged and picked up another log. "Go home, relax, and don't worry too much about what Reverend Williams said."

He then jumped and lifted his foot.

"Ouch!" As he held his foot, I saw a feral rat scurry away. "I think something bit my toe."

"Are you okay?" I looked at his foot.

"I'll be alright. Only a little blood. Go home and relax. You look like you've been working hard since this morning." He put his hand on my shoulder and gave a wolfish grin. "When I come home," he whispered, "I'll fix dinner. Okay?"

"Well, that does sound nice." I purred softly. "Okay. I'll head home. Stay safe." I waved goodbye to him and started walking home.

The torches were lit in the town, and few people roamed the streets. I didn't hear any wolves as I treaded through the fields, which was unusual. The silence made me more nervous than the howling. As I got home, I took my shoes off and untied my shirt. I sat down and gave a tired sigh. It was good to get off my feet. However, I felt a fresh wave of anxiety as I thought about Thomas.

I began to nod off waiting for the wolf. *Maybe if I just sleep for a moment*, I thought, *time might pass quicker.* I fell asleep at the table.

As I woke back up some time later, I saw Thomas entering the kitchen. I yawned and looked up at him.

"Good morning," he said as he smiled at me and raised an eyebrow. "Judging by your head fur, you slept well?"

"Morning?" I asked as I jumped up. "I slept all night?" I brushed my head a few times with my hands and went up to the bedroom to change. As I came back out, I saw that Thomas was struggling to undress. It looked like he grew, his clothes tighter than I remembered.

"Do you need any help?" I asked even as I untied his shirt.

"Thank you," he replied. "Feels like my clothes shrank." He finally managed to take his shirt off and looked at it. I noticed that he was more muscular than before, his arms and torso grown out.

"Have you been spending extra time working?" I tilted my head in confusion. I gave his arms a squeeze, feeling how hard they were. "Oh my…"

"Well, that's what working at the mill does, I suppose," he replied with a blush, and chuckled. He flexed his muscles a bit and shrugged.

"Not just that. You've…grown?" I looked up at him, and then looked at his pants to see that the legs only reached his ankles. He tried to sit down, and I heard a rip. "Umm, you might want to take those off first." He chuckled and nodded as he took his pants off. I scanned him up and down.

"Are you sure you don't want me to disrobe just for your pleasure?" he asked as he got closer to me, then wrapped an arm around me. "You needn't but ask."

"Oh shut it, you." I laughed and playfully pushed him.

He let go of me as he groaned and held his head. "Sorry. My head is hurting for some reason. I feel a little dizzy, too." He sat down and I rubbed his temples. "Mmm, that doesn't help with the dizziness, but it is helping with the headache." He chuckled and murred softly. "Thank you, dear." He took my long tail and nuzzled it. "I might just take a nap before I go."

"Nonsense, Tom. You're not going to work today. You need to rest. They're probably overworking you there. Go to bed." I noticed him shivering. "Go. I'll bring you something later, okay?"

"You're too good to me, Ed. Thank you." He smiled, nodded, and headed to bed.

I decided to go back into the fields and harvest more wheat. Clouds started gathering, and the wolves were silent. I picked wheat for a few hours before it started to rain and I went back inside. Hearing Thomas whine, I made some soup for him to eat in bed, then entered the bedroom to see him waking up. He tossed and turned, growling.

"Thomas, are you okay?" I felt his head; it was hot to the touch. I ran into the kitchen and wet a cloth, then dabbed it on his head. "Easy."

"Thank you, Ed." He smiled up at me and murred as he rubbed my arm. "You always know how to make me feel better."

"Shh, just rest. Here." I sat him up and fed him a spoonful of egg and vegetable soup, then put it on the table next to his bed. "Listen, I have to go back out before it begins to rain again, okay? Rest and eat your soup." We exchanged smiles. The sun was setting as I headed out, but it was brighter since the clouds had scattered. The moon and stars were out again. The wolves' howls didn't even bother me, as I was too hypnotized by the dark blue sky.

After a little while stargazing, I finished gathering the wheat and brought it inside. I headed toward the bedroom.

"Tom, I'm back. How are you—" The room was empty. "Tom?" As I looked around the house, I called again. "Thomas? Where are you?" He couldn't be anywhere in the house; there weren't many places to hide in our small hovel. I stepped back outside and saw a beastlike figure running through the fields. It dropped something as it ran; the pants that Thomas had ripped. *I wonder if…hmm that can't be right. Just a myth.* "I hope you're okay, Thomas," I said.

As foolish as it was, I ventured into the woods. The wolves' howls grew louder and were accompanied with growls. They startled me, but knowing that Tom might be in danger kept me moving. *Perhaps he went into the woods to escape the beast*, I thought.

As I looked for signs of him among the dark trees, a pair of glowing blue eyes appeared within the bushes, stopping me in my tracks. A snarl came from their direction, so I turned and walked another direction. Eventually, the sound of footsteps drew near as I heard the same snarl. Walking faster, the footsteps seemed to fade behind me.

As I ended up back in the fields, I looked behind me and saw nothing. *Back where I started?* I sighed and chuckled, thinking it was just my imagination. I turned back around and bumped into a two-legged, bulky beast. In the moonlight, it had dark grey fur and the blue eyes I had seen before. It gave a menacing growl like in the forest and pounced on me, pinning me down. Drool hung from its gaping maw. As I looked into its eyes, they looked more personified than I expected. Its eyes expressed sadness, reminding me of Thomas' eyes when he saw little Susan hanged.

"Thomas?" I asked, looking up at him. He replied with a soft whine as he sat down next to me. It seemed that his animalistic instincts had taken over. "How did this happen? Is this...lycanthropy?" He showed me the toe that the rat had bitten. It was a dark red.

"That rat bite did that to you? That can't be." I mused as I looked at his toe. "Or perhaps it was a carrier..." He looked down and whined some more. He then lifted his head and howled at the moon. I tried to stifle him by closing his mouth. "Easy!" He seemed to understand me, since he stopped howling. "Do you know what people would do if they found you like this?" I rubbed his head softly, then gave him a hug as he panted and rested his head against mine.

I felt something poke at my thigh. Thomas's face was a dark red beneath the fur it had sprouted as he looked away.

"Tom, are you...?" I rubbed his thigh as I saw his cock growing from his sheath. "Heh, I see you are." He panted more.

Before I knew it, my arms were pinned to the ground. His eyes looked more like a feral wolf's, peering into mine. He raised a hand. As he bared his claws, he swung down and sliced my shirt open, then clawed off my pants.

"E-easy, Thomas!" I said as I stood back up, completely nude. "I don't have much clothing that you can just ruin, you know." I looked around and found myself caught in his grasp as he held me from behind. He began to rub my torso and fondle my sheath; my cock grew hard beneath his touch. He couldn't have lost all of his humanity; he wasn't feral. He then turned me around, and I felt his warm drool seep from his maw and onto my face.

He began to lick at my muzzle, slipping his big tongue into my maw. I gasped and moaned, though it was muffled as he began kissing me deeply. I didn't resist for some reason, as though I wasn't of sound mind. Our tongues wrestled around in each other's mouths. I felt his huge, erect cock press against me. One beastlike hand ran down my body, the other curled around the back of my head. I shivered and moaned in pleasure.

I tried to resist, but my body kept fighting my mind. I began leaking pre-cum as my cock throbbed in Tom's hand. If he kept this up, I would climax soon.

Tom stopped fondling me and pushed me down on all fours. He stuck his finger into my tight hole and made me moan. I felt his claws dig into my back.

"T-Tom, that hurts. Ow! It feels like you're scraping inside me," I whined, though he didn't let up for long moments. He finally pulled his finger out, only to slide his huge cock against my tail. I looked back to see how big it really was.

"Tom, are you sure that'll fi–ohhh!" I let out a moan as he pushed his cock into me. I've never felt such a sensation of pain and pleasure in my life. I couldn't help but moan again and again. It hurt so much, but so good.

Tom held me against him, wrapping an arm around my neck and thrusting deeply.

"T-Tom," I cried out, "This feels…so amazing!" I continued moaning as I reached back and rubbed his cheek. He licked at my throat and bared his fangs. As he sunk them into my shoulder, I felt a tear in my eye, though I was overwhelmed by bliss.

He rolled onto his back, bringing me on top of him. He thrusted quicker as he panted and growled. I was getting used to his huge cock inside me, and began to reciprocate.

"That's it, Tom. Deeper…harder!" He seemed to understand me, as he did just that. My eyes started to roll back; I felt nothing but pleasure. My tongue lolled out as I felt his against the back of my neck. "I'm so close!"

My toes curled as he thrusted harder. I felt his knot pound against my entrance, swollen with his lust. My legs shook as he growled, and I shuddered with ecstasy. He throbbed harder as he managed to push his knot inside me. He let out a loud howl as he released his hot lupine spunk inside me.

Feeling his hot seed inside me sent me over the edge. I shot my seed all over us as he thrusted and snarled softly beneath me. He nuzzled my head against his and slowly pulled out.

"I love you, Thomas," I said as I looked at him. I saw his eyes turn back into the soft orbs of beautiful blue that I knew so well. He kept his arms around me. I turned onto my front and cuddled with the soft, fluffy lycan. All of the pleasure from the climax made my muscles go limp. I closed my eyes and slept on Tom's broad, muscular frame.

As I slept, I started hearing Reverend Williams's voice. "Edmund. Edmund?" he called. "Edmund!"

I woke up to find myself in my bed, a book hanging off it.

"Ed," Thomas said, lying beside me. "You've been growling in your sleep again." He chuckled as I grabbed the book and put it on the table.

"Oh, it was…" I looked at him, inspecting his body. He seemed normal.

"Enjoying yourself?" he asked as he raised an eyebrow.

"It was all a dream? You're not a lycan?"

"If I am, I'm quite the civilized one. Let's see." He took the book. "*The Beast Within: Further Studies in Lycanthropy?* That explains it." He chuckled and put the book back on the table. "Stop reading these types of books. Nothing but a bunch of 'I found tracks' and stories about someone's friend looking different. They'll keep you up—or more importantly, me. Little Susan's getting released from prison, yet they might put her on the noose tomorrow."

"Sorry, Tom. I'll try to keep quiet." I gave him a warm smile. Without hesitation, the words slipped from me. "I love you."

"What?" His eyes opened wide.

"Goodnight!" I blew out the candle and went to sleep.

Stowaway
Transatlantic - 1703 CE

The salty sea air, the shanties sung by the deckhands, the beautiful view from the crow's nest, and traversing rigorous storms were but a few reasons I enjoyed sailing. The sound of waves brushing up against the ship and the occasional gulls squawking were music to my fox ears.

Being a stowaway, however, my luxuries on the ship were limited. I did not want to risk being killed for some pleasant sounds and an even more pleasant view. I just wanted to get to England alive. I always thought of myself as a patient one, but I couldn't wait an extra week to see my grandmother, or else it might be too late. I was not about to go back on my promise to see her this summer.

I heard someone shouting commands, most likely the captain or first mate. I could not make out much of what he said from inside my barrel; everything was muffled. After a few hours sitting in the barrel, my stomach growled like a ravenous beast. We were going to be at sea for days, I assumed. I did not think I would be able to last the whole trip without anything to eat or drink.

I poked my head out, ears twitching. Looking at the barrels and supplies and small bed, I assumed it was a supply room. Nobody was in sight. As I hopped out of the barrel, a splinter snagged onto my vest and ripped it. I looked at the tear and sighed. *This is going to be a long trip.* I searched around the small, dingy cabin for something to eat. "Nothing? Not even bread?"

I groaned, as I rifled through a dresser. I looked under the bed and inside another barrel. "Nothing," I whispered and shook my head. As I continued my aimless search, I heard footsteps on the wooden floor outside the cabin. I rushed back into the barrel, but the splintering wood snagged onto my vest again. There was a slight crack in the barrel that I could peek through. The footsteps came closer to the room, and a shadow appeared outside the doorway. A rough-looking greenish-gray rat entered with a low soft growl. His left ear looked as if something had bitten into it.

He sat down, his thin, bandaged tail swaying to one side. As he adjusted his boots, he picked up something. It was a brown piece of leather, like my vest. I looked at it to see a piece had ripped from it. I hadn't realized it had torn that much.

The rat glanced around the room as his nose twitched, taking in the scent of the leather. An inquisitive hum came from his muzzle as he sniffed near the cot, and then at the small wooden table. He came closer to the barrel, but then turned away and continued searching.

As I gave a relieved sigh, he turned around, his ears twitching. *Damn.* I covered my mouth as he trudged closer to the barrel. He sniffed at it and gave a raspy groan.

"Come on out, you," said the rat as he drew his sword.

I slowly emerged from the barrel. As I climbed out, the rat took me in his arms. He spun me around, one hand holding my hands behind me as the other held his sword to my throat.

"Easy!" I said as I struggled a bit. "Watch the tail."

"Shut up, intruder!" he replied with a raspy voice. He kept his sword at my neck, almost touching my skin. "What are you doing here, huh? Have you come to steal our supplies? Seize the ship for yourself?"

"I was just…I just wanted to get to England," I replied as I kept struggling. Although, what was the point? No matter what I said, my life was finished here.

"Hmm…" He lowered his sword and turned me around, looking me over. "No weapons, I see." He patted me down. A jingle of coins could be heard from my pocket.

"How much?" I asked as I pulled out my coin pouch. "I just want to see my grandmother, sir."

"I neither want nor need your coin, stranger." He crossed his arms and raised an eyebrow. "That wouldn't be enough, anyway." He circled around me like a vulture. "I should toss you overboard, but we could use another deckhand. You certainly look the part." He fiddled with my vest and loose trousers.

"A deckhand?" I retorted. "I just wanted to get to England."

"You'd rather swim there? You came onto our vessel without permission. Do you expect a trip of luxury? Servants at your feet? Food in your mouth?"

I gave it a moment's thought. I knew he was being facetious, but the image of being waited on made me chuckle.

"You think this is a joke, stranger? You're not a guest," he continued. "You will work with the crew: hoisting the mainsail, manning the lifeboats, and other duties. You'll be treated just like any other deckhand."

"I... I don't know what to say," I replied. I looked away for a moment and gave a thoughtful hum.

"Will you accept?"

"There can't be any way that you would do this for me for no payment." I crossed my arms and raised an eyebrow.

"Well, since you'll be disguising yourself as a deckhand, you don't want people to know you're a stowaway, right? I'll keep your secret..." he said, putting his hand on my shoulder, "...for a price."

"What price?" I felt his warm breath close to my ear, and heard a gentle chuckle.

"Well, have you been dirty with a man, fox?" He continued to circle me. I responded with a cautious nod and noticed the frigid glare from the rat's narrowed red eyes, one having a scar over it. "This ship is full of...depraved men and no women, including myself. Sure, they like to pleasure themselves, and each other on occasion. I want more, however. It gets monotonous." He sighed and shook his head. "Surely you must know what I mean by now." He sat on another barrel, looking up at me.

"This ship is full of depraved men, as you said. Why not pleasure yourself with them?"

"I've been sailing with these louts for years on end." He leaned against the wall, hands behind his head. "It'd be nice to have something, well, new."

"Well, I…" I felt a warmness spreading on my face.

"Your cheeks are blood red, fox. Was it something I said?" he asked as he sat back up. Looking at his bare chest, he had quite the physique. He could have been worse. Much to my shame, I nodded. "So we have a deal, then? You work for the ship and you keep your life?"

"Yes," I replied with slight hesitation.

"And you do some work for me…and your secret stays safe?"

"Yes," I replied with even more hesitation. "If I can see my grandmother, then yes."

"Lovely." He gave a slight smile as he stood up. "Let's go." He led me up to the deck. "You can call me Scartail, by the way."

"Scartail?" I raised an eyebrow at the peculiar name.

"Yes, Scartail," he responded forcefully. "Yourself?"

"Samuel, sir."

"Well, 'Samuel sir,' that's bloody boring. I'll call you Foxy." He put his hand on my shoulder and gave a toothy grin. "Let me show you around." Foxy didn't sound much better than Samuel, but I supposed everyone had their own nicknames. I was sure Scartail wasn't his real name either.

The sun nearly blinded me as we walked. I heard the high-pitched cries of seagulls. It was intoxicating. The giant sails blowing, the waves hitting the sides of the ship, and the beautiful view of the horizon was tantalizing. I felt like I was home. I wasn't in my own home, however; I was in someone else's. I was a trespasser, not a guest. As with any trespasser, I could be killed, and nobody would bat an eye.

The only thing that kept me from being tossed in the sea was Scartail. I stayed close to him. What else was I going to do—go off on my own? I didn't want to risk the consequences.

I heard a shantyman start another song. "When I was a little lad and so me mother told me..." he sang as he started pulling on a rope in rhythm with the song.

"Way haul away, we'll haul away Joe," they responded as they pulled as well.

"Haul Away Joe," Scartail said as we walked. "An old favorite."

"That if I did not kiss the girls me lips would grow all moldy," continued the shantyman.

"Way haul away, we'll haul away Joe!" This time, Scartail joined in as well with his gruff voice.

"You're not much of a singer, are you?" I joked.

"I'd curb that tongue if I were you, boy," he replied with a soft snarl. I stepped back and put my hands up. Perhaps he didn't have a sense of humor? They continued to sing. "We like to sing at times," said the rat. "Being on the open sea for days on end can be tiring."

"Tiring?" I opened my eyes wide. "But you're out at sea! You couldn't be freer exploring the oceans."

"We may be 'free', but that doesn't mean it doesn't get boring from time to time, Foxy." I still could not fathom how life at sea could be boring. "Or were you a layabout when you sailed?" He smirked and put a hand on his hip. "Listen to them singing."

I nodded and listened to their song: *Way haul away, we'll haul away Joe!* Though joyful, their tones had a hint of fatigue, most likely due to long days of working with little rest.

"Now enough of the introduction," Scartail said. "This ain't a tour, fox. Time to put you to work, swabbie."

"Wait, what?" I suddenly had a mop tossed at me. I looked at it with a raised eyebrow.

"Not good enough for ya, boy?" Scartail looked at me as he crossed his arms. "You're not trying to call attention to yourself, right? Unless you'd rather be the barnacle boy? You know what that is, don't ya?" Knowing exactly what that was, I looked away, unresponsive. He smirked and chuckled. "Good, now get swabbing."

I sighed and started swabbing the deck. I expected to be put to some sort of work, so I couldn't complain. It could have been worse: Scartail could've had me scraping barnacles from the ship's underside. There wasn't much I could do but follow his orders. So, I swabbed and swabbed. The others left me alone. I assumed they thought that a swabbie wasn't worth talking to. That didn't matter though; the important thing was that I was headed to England.

As the sun began to rest on the horizon, I noticed that many of the riggers and deckhands went down to the mess deck. I stayed above and leaned over the side of the boat. I sighed, resting my head on the ship's railing as I watched the sun disappear.

"Ah, the cool summer night's breeze," said the helmsman as he smiled up at the stars. "I love manning the helm at night. Peaceful, quiet solitude." He then looked at me. "Don't mind me lad; just thinking aloud."

"There you are," said Scartail as he came up from below. "Beautiful, isn't it?"

I nodded; as I watched the waves crash, a dolphin chittered and sprung from the water. I looked up to the stars twinkling in the sky.

"I love coming out here at night," he said as he leaned his back toward the edge. "It eases the mind. Gets me away from all that hustle and bustle on the mess deck."

"That's what I told him!" said the ship's helmsman as he let out a hearty laugh.

"We're going to my quarters. You thought I'd forget about *our* part of the deal, boy?" He smirked as we walked. "Some relaxing would be needed after a hard day's work, anyway." He gently pushed me into his quarters and shut the door behind him. It was smaller than I imagined, though there was enough room for a bed, night stand, and table. "You're quite the handsome stowaway, I'll admit."

I wanted to say the same to him, but I was trying not to drool as he began to untie his tunic, showing his toned chest and broad shoulders. My blood started rushing, and I tried fanning myself with my vest. As he removed his tunic, I couldn't help but stare in awe at his sculpted midsection that offset his ragged grey fur, a few scars here and there complimenting his figure.

I'd never been with a rat before. I wasn't about to pass up an opportunity with such a masculine and messy companion. Why was I so aroused, though? He was not the most appealing of people, but his dominant attitude made my trousers tighten.

The rat reached out, snaking his hand inside my brown vest. I exhaled deeply at the sensation of his strong fingers against my chest. "Quite the physique on you, if I say so myself, Foxy." All I could retort with was a chuckle and flushed cheeks.

Scartail removed his hand from beneath my vest, and began unbuttoning it. He leaned in to place a soft kiss right at the deepest part of the V over my chest, where the cloth of the vest lapped over itself to button shut. He moved his muzzle up to my neck and kissed there. I let out a soft moan, and my tail swayed. Taking a whiff of his musk had aroused me even more.

His fingers opened another button, and another, as the deckhand relieved me of my top. I rested my hands on his burly shoulders, clutching at them just to see if they were as firm as I had imagined. I had imagined right. Another soft moan escaped my maw as the rat kissed my neck again. He pulled me closer and cupped my behind in his powerful deckhand hands.

The rat looked at me with his sinister crimson eyes and unbuckled my belt, then slipped my trousers down to the floor. Fully naked now, and sporting an erecting member, I couldn't hide my arousal. I decided to interact instead of just watch; my hands made my way to his trousers and unbuckled his belt.

I gently pushed him back a bit, pressing him against a wall. As his trousers dropped to the floor, I pressed against the rat's toned figure.

"Looks like you're enjoying this as well," he said with a chuckle.

"Perhaps," I replied, blushing as I realized that we were both baring it all in a matter of minutes.

"Show me what that muzzle can do, Foxy." His eyes narrowed as he licked his lips slowly.

I took him up on his request and brought our muzzles together in a tender kiss. The rat's hand found its way immediately to my crotch, rolling his palm up my furry sac, making me moan softly and submissively within my chest. I rested my palms against the toned chest of the rat, caressing the framed musculature. The sensation of the rat's erection pressing against my own hard member made them both throb, making me release a shaky sigh.

He took his hand off my member to grope my rear, running his hand over my round rump. He continued to rub it slowly while planting his tongue inside my maw. I ran my fingers through his unkempt shoulder-length brown hair, letting out a soft murr as his mouth pressed against mine. As we parted lips I couldn't help voicing one question on my mind. It slipped past my lips.

"How are we going to…you know…?" I looked down at our throbbing members and blushed a bit. "Do you want me to…or do you want to…?"

The rat actually blushed as well before answering. I could barely see it in the dim light. It was rather out of place, I thought, to see a scruffy rat like him get flustered.

"Actually," he finally said with a look to the side, "I prefer to 'grab the sheets'…if you'll forgive the language." That made me tilt my head. I wasn't sure if that meant he was dominant or submissive. "You don't know what that means?" he asked with a sigh. I shook my head. "I like to receive, boy." That caught me off-guard, given his demeanor. Perhaps Scartail took notice of my reaction. "I know, I know. However, I'll have you know that lots of men on this ship would rather receive than give; it's what I enjoy. All the same…there was something else I wanted to do first," the rat finished, lifting me up off my feet. I gasped at his strength, curious what it was he had in store for me.

"Though before we can do that," he said with lustful red eyes.

"What do you—" Before I had the chance to finish my question, the rat began slipping his tongue against my lips and pushing it into my maw. His wet cock slid against mine. So, that's what he meant by fun. I couldn't argue with that. Gasps and moans left us between each kiss.

After our tongues had thoroughly wrestled, he broke the kiss. He slid his tongue down the midline of my body, giving an occasional nuzzle. He kissed my stomach, then made his way lower, licking above my crotch. His crimson eyes peered up at me as he ran his tongue up the length of my cock. I bit my lip as he slid my erection into his maw.

He swirled his long wet rodent tongue around my girth. I gasped sharply, the sensation of my full length being taken with such swift ease sending a tingle up my spine. All I could do was take in the pleasure he gave. Eight inches of my cock sank into the maw of an eager rat, his hands bracing against my rump to hold me in place while he took the rat's fill.

My head tilted back occasionally, as I took to rocking my hips in time with the bobbing of Scartail's head. My thrusting grew more pronounced, more quickly feeding my manhood into the rat's hungry muzzle. I put my hand on his head, grabbing his unkempt black hair. I had never experienced this kind of sexual bliss before, as I'd always been on the receiving end. It was still hard to believe that a manly rat like him was into fancies like this, along with other deckhands. I had assumed they were far too proud and masculine to do anything submissive.

Time had ceased for me. How long had we been doing this? Was he going to keep going until I hit my climax? Even as the thought crossed my mind, he pulled back from my wet member, leaving it coated in his warm saliva. I couldn't help panting a little. He rose to his feet and pressed his muzzle against mine. This time, he let out a moan as we kissed, our tongues playing with each other. He soon broke the kiss and raised an eyebrow at me.

"Well…?" he asked. "On your knees, boy. I'm getting some service as well." He pushed me down, forcing me to kneel before him, slapping my face with his hard member, then pressing it against my muzzle. I opened my maw for his thick rathood, and with a grunt he eagerly pushed it in. I already tasted his warm pre spilling out, lapping it up slowly. He began giving slow thrusts into my maw, gripping at my head fur.

"That's it, Foxy," he said with a lustful groan. "Take it like a good boy."

I continued sucking on him, his cock throbbing and leaking more pre in my mouth. Panting through his nose, he thrusted deeper and poked at the back of my throat, causing me to choke, though it was muffled by my mouth being full of his cock. His moans deepened, and he soon pulled out, his member now lubed with my saliva. I eagerly lapped at the tip, wanting more of his taste, but he stopped me and pulled me to my feet.

"That's enough, boy," he said. He pushed me to the foot of his bed. He lay down on his back, stretching out and smirking up at me.

"Don't be shy," he said as he pulled me by my hand. I ended up on top of the rat, straddling him. Heeding his words, I closed the distance between us and planted a soft kiss on his muzzle. He licked mine in return, wrapping his arms around me. He rested on one arm as he propped himself up with the other, letting him deepen the kiss. He raised his hips up until my tip pressed against his entrance. I felt his long, thin tail flick against mine, then start to coil around it. There was a twinkle in his eye, as if he was telling me that he was ready for me to enter.

"Take me, Foxy. I want you inside me." That was all I needed to hear from him.

I pressed my tip past his entrance, sinking my length into him, causing the rat to let out a gasping moan. Scartail was larger than me by any measure. I gave a soft chuckle at the situation.

"What ya laughing at, Foxy?" He chuckled with me and caressed my cheek.

"I'm used to the larger person being on top."

"First time for everything, eh? Now let's see what you can do, boy."

That was my cue. I began thrusting into him, pulling his hips closer to me.

He took my girth with ease. Was I not big enough? Even someone with experience in receiving should still provide a bit of resistance. However, given the deep submissive moaning and groaning I heard, I was assured that I was doing well. He took my full eight inches, so I gave it to him again and again.

Lying over him, I felt his throbbing cock press against my stomach. The sensation made me moan in pleasure. Catching a hint of his arousing scent helped as well. I pressed my muzzle to the hairy pit of his arm. The musk was strong and made my cock pulse even harder. I thrusted faster as he wrapped an arm around my neck. He curled his free hand around his member and began stroking.

As our scents mixed together, my hips smacked against his rump. I heard the rhythmic creaking of the bedframe drowning out our soft moans and labored breathing. I began to growl as I thrusted, coating his passage with pre and making my shaft slicker, my thrusts faster.

I paced myself, as I didn't want to finish too fast. He seemed to enjoy me being inside him, and I didn't want to ruin that. I went slower to resist my climax. His, however, seemed to be coming closer. I pinned his hands to the bed, our fingers interlocked and our lips pressed together.

"Wait," he interrupted, much to my surprise. "Pull out."

Against my deeper desires, I obliged and slowly pulled my foxhood from the rat, then climbed off him. He pushed me onto my back, and began licking at my hole. I gasped as he rimmed me, clenching the bedsheets and curling my toes. He pressed his tongue past my entrance and into my rear. I held the sheets tighter as he licked inside me, gasping in pleasure.

He eventually slid his tongue from my hole. My cock was still fully hard as he brushed his nose up against my balls, taking in my scent. He gave a content hum as he moved up and gave my member a slow lick.

"Tasty fox," he said as he climbed on top of me and gave me a deep kiss, licking inside my maw. He pressed his hole against my shaft once again, slipping the tip inside of him. I groaned softly, as he sank onto my eager cock.

He pressed my hands down to the bed. I could do nothing but hump into him and moan. He pushed against my groin in time with my thrusts. Occasionally he would flex his toned body. He gave deep lustful breaths as beads of sweat formed on his forehead and chest. I wrapped my arms around him, pulling the rat against me, enjoying his slick body against mine. I groaned out as he nibbled and sucked on my neck. The sensations had me throbbing harder inside his warm passage. I ran my hands up and down his powerful back, each muscle flexing against my hands. It felt amazing.

"If I didn't know any better, I'd think this were more intimate than just pleasure." I smirked up at him as I ran my hands down his sides.

"You think?" He winced a bit at the pain complementing the pleasure. "Well, don't get too comfortable here, boy. Once I'm finished, it's back to the mess deck with you." He smirked as he continued riding my shaft.

As we kept going, I leaked more pre-cum inside him, as did his own as he started stroking himself. My breathing became heavier as my tongue lolled out. I heard the rat's breathing becoming harsher also. With both hands, Tails grabbed onto a beam. He began thrusting harder against my crotch, letting out groans and grunts.

As his passage was working my shaft, I pulled his hand away and wrapped my own around his cock and began stroking it in time with his thrusts. He took my length with ease, his rump slapping my groin each time he hilted himself on me. Those wonderful sounds were music to my twitching ears.

Swimming in my ecstasy, my chest heaved, and my panting grew more ragged. My balls tightened as the scents of our sex became intoxicating; I felt like I was in a trance. I wrapped my arms around his back once more, propping my body up against his. Our strong scents mixed together as I pressed my nose under his arm, the scraggly hairs brushing against my muzzle. The musk of a working man was more enticing than any perfume.

The words that the rat spoke as he plunged himself on top of me just spurred me on. "Mm...how do you like the smell, boy? Good, ain't it?" I could only respond with an eager nod. "You like fucking me like this, don't ya?" I said yes with a lustful hum as I thrusted in unison with him.

Scartail murred softly as his pre-cum streamed onto my stomach. I began stroking his cock with some of his pre on my hand, making it nice and slick. His shaft was throbbing hard in my hand as I rubbed it more quickly. The bed started creaking with our movements. I thrusted harder and harder and saw his chest heaving as well. From the rat's heavy panting, I could tell his climax was drawing near as well.

"I'm almost there, boy," he said as he groaned in pleasure. He leaned down to kiss me as I wrapped my free arm around his back once more.

"Me too, Scartail," I grunted out as we continued. I felt the pleasure building up inside me. "What should I—"

"Cum...cum inside me. Breed me."

With that, I shut my eyes, hearing his moans and squeaking as pre-cum kept dripping from his tip. I throbbed inside of him as he bounced on my cock, his erection hitting my stomach each time. I looked up at him, watching him slam onto my crotch, groaning louder each time. I couldn't hold back anymore, driven over the edge by his arousing musk and tight passage squeezing around me. I gave a few forceful thrusts into him, releasing my seed inside Scartail, gasping out as he clenched around my throbbing member. Panting heavily, I became nearly lightheaded. My balls twitched as a steady stream of my seed continued to fill his hole, some of it spilling down my shaft and some trailing down the rat's behind. His own balls rested on my stomach.

"You haven't…released yet," I managed to say through my panting.

"I wanted you to first." He smirked, his eyes mesmerizing as he looked down at me.

"And now…?" I raised an eyebrow at the rat. He lifted himself off my member and licked the spunk off it. He then kissed me, giving me a taste of my own seed.

As we kissed, he moved between my legs and spread them. "Now it's my turn." He licked his lips, his eyes half-lidded. I tilted my head. "I said I like to receive. Doesn't mean I don't like to be on the giving end occasionally." The new view of him was just as amazing. The rat pinned my hands and kneeled over me, showing his dominance; he must have realized my interest in that.

He showed no hesitation in entering my passage, making me gasp and moan at how swiftly he penetrated me. He began slow, smooth thrusts as I grew used to his member. As I relaxed around him, he picked up the pace of his movements. Groaning out, he wrapped his arms around me. I curled my legs around his waist as he picked me up, still on his knees. I grabbed onto the beam above us as he pumped into me, his member throbbing inside me. He leaked more pre, making my passage slick, and thrust quicker.

I took every inch with ease, trembling in pleasure. He pressed his nose under my arm, inhaling deeply. I felt the tip of his tongue licking at my pit. His groans grew louder and more heavy, hinting that he was nearing his climax. He pulled his head from under my arm and gave me an intense look—a look of anger and power, as though he were feral. Soon enough, he let out a loud growl, holding me tight and releasing his seed deep inside my passage. His eyes rolled back as his tongue lolled out. I panted heavily as he filled me to the brim with his warm rodent spunk.

He let me go, allowing me to rest on my back. He collapsed on top of me, our chests heaving against each other. I felt hot, dizzy, relaxed, and happy all at the same time. I slowly wrapped an arm around his back as he gently rubbed his cheek against mine. He gradually pulled out of me and gave me a deep and passionate kiss.

"I needed that," he whispered in my ear. "Thank you, Foxy." He had a satisfied glow.

I chuckled softly, not sure what to say. "Anytime," is all I could think of. "You act like you've never been handled like that before."

"I might as well be honest with you, boy," he explained. "Besides the cap'n and another deckhand who had his arse thrown overboard, I haven't been with anyone else on the ship. The others are usually occupied with other affairs, or their work... or other men." Hearing that surprised me. "Nobody wants a dirty rat."

"You don't look any dirtier than anyone else on this ship." I chuckled softly.

"I'm not, really," he replied with a chuckle of his own. "But that's the first thing they think of when they see a rat: diseases. Who would want to lay with someone with a disease?" He sighed and shook his head. He got off of me and sat at the edge of the bed. "Go on ahead, boy. I'll keep your secret. You have my word as a sailor. I'm not going to force you into anything."

I sympathized with the rat. I wanted to leave but my legs weren't letting me. I sat next to him instead. "It hurts." I looked at him. "The rumors (or reputations); that's all they see. They assume I'll just bed anyone. I've caught people looking as if I was a demon of lust. The only reason I bedded you was because...well, you blackmailed me." I chuckled and shrugged. "Not that I didn't enjoy the encounter."

He laughed as we both started getting dressed. "Well, you should probably get back down to the mess—"

"You know," I interrupted. "I wouldn't mind doing this again." I gave him a wink and smiled.

"Why?" He looked as if he couldn't believe his ears.

"Because we had a deal, remember? I do some work for you, you keep my secret. I believe I shall hold up my end of the bargain. It's only fair, don't you think?"

"I can't argue with that," the rat replied with a chuckle. He wrapped his hands and tail around my waist and gave me a soft kiss. He then turned away, possibly to hide his blush.

"I'll be back." I smiled and returned his kiss. "Until tomorrow."

I left his quarters to see the moon shining brightly over the sea. I saw the helmsman at his post, smiling down at me.

"Enjoy yourself with the rodent?" he asked.

"I did." I nodded and smiled. "I really did."

I enjoyed my moment of solitude, looking out to the horizon and feeling the sea air breeze against my face. What I expected to be a trip of hiding or being thrown overboard turned into an enjoyable one.

El Juego
Granátula de Calatrava, Spain - 1821 CE

The life of a noble can either be a very long one or very short one, depending on how you play the game. It can also be an exciting one where you'll see assassinations at assemblies, or it can be boring, where you sit on your laurels behind closed doors. One can be feared, loved, or hated, as long as one is known. Sadly, I am not one of those nobles. My name is Don Joaquín Baldomero Fernández-Espartero y Alvarez de la Patilla, viscount of Banderas—or simply Don Baldomero. It didn't feel like enough. I still felt like a commoner among nobles. I wanted more. I needed more. Being the last of nine children was like being the pup among wolves…literally.

In my estate, I paced back and forth in my room and looked in my mirror. "Baldomero," I asked my reflection, "What are you going to do with yourself? Your life is nothing but a bore and ruin." I paused then chuckled. "Perhaps I could start with clothing myself." I wagged my tail, looking at myself in my undergarments. I then got dressed and exited my bedroom.

Going downstairs, a message on table next to the steps stopped me. *La fiesta empieza a esta noche a las diez. Come to my estate, mi amigo.* I would recognize the penmanship from anywhere. Marquis Ronaldo, de San Lorenzo del Valleumbroso, a longtime friend, always threw parties for the nobility. As I left my estate, I heard my servant rush out the front door.

"Señor! Señor!" she called as she reached me. She put my handkerchief in my shirt pocket. "My apologies; you almost forgot."

"Not a problem," I said with a smile. "Gracias. As you were, Nadia."

I straightened my outfit, then left for the marketplace. The sun kept the town warm during the day. The market was always loud and musical. One could always hear a vendor advertising their wares: "Fresh meat! Fine silk! Gold imported jewelry!" It became quite an earsore for me. Instead of walking through the market, I just went into the Marsella to get something to eat. It was much quieter than the market, despite the occasional fights that happened. Even the fights were entertaining, however.

The smell of tapas as well as ale filled the air in the Marsella. Unusually, I noticed Ronaldo at the bar, slumped over with a small empty glass and scratching his horns.

"Ronaldo?" I called as I went over to him. "What are you doing here? I didn't know you drink." He turned his head my way as he heard me call out to him.

"Oh, Baldomero, mi amigo!" the bull greeted cheerfully as he raised his empty glass. "Come, take a seat. Have a drink on me. Another round, barman." He snapped his fingers. The bartender came by with two glasses and set them down.

I sat down next to him and grabbed a glass. The strong fruity scent of tequila pierced my nostrils like a needle.

"Quite strong," I said, coughing from the stench.

"That's when you know it's good, my friend." He let out a loud guffaw and slapped my back. "It's the finest tequila in Banderas."

"You would know, wouldn't you, Toro?" I took a swig of my drink as it burned going down, causing me to make disgusted faces.

"Damn right I would, perrito! Also good for drowning out tears, no?"

"What do you mean?" I tilted my head as he put his glass down and looked at me with puffy, red eyes. He looked as though he had been crying for hours.

"Valentina," he replied. "Perhaps, I should say the bitch that crushed my heart."

"Oh, I'm so sorry, Ronaldo. I didn't…"

"I gave that snake everything!" he shouted, "And she just…" He groaned and put his head on the table.

"Snake? She cheated on you, Ronaldo?" I asked.

"No, she was an actual snake—a wonderful woman with beautiful scales." He shook his head as he looked at his half-empty glass and shook the drink around. "She tempted me with her lovely purple eyes. 'Ronaldo,' she said. 'Eres mi corazón!' Yesterday, I saw her in some lizard's arms, completely bare. His disgusting hands all over her body, caressing her…"

"You needn't go on. I understand." I put my hand on his shoulder.

He smiled and chuckled. "It's not the first time she did it, nor the second." He looked at me with a smirk. "The eighth. Octavo vez! Eight!" I noticed other people starting to glance at him as he grew louder. He was about to take another drink, but I put a hand on his hand.

"Relax, hombre. I think you've had enough for today," I said as I noticed that he was wobbling on his stool. I helped him down and paid the barman.

"You're a good friend, Baldo," he said with a slurred voice. I could barely make out what he was saying. He then chuckled. "Baldo, but you have fur on your head. Ha! Tienes pelo." He started rubbing my head and leaned against me. I helped the wobbly bull find his way home. Occasionally he burst into random song.

As we entered his estate, one of the maids gasped. "My lord! Is he alright?"

I laughed and nodded. "Just had a bit much to drink. I'll take him to bed." With Ronaldo, at times I felt like a mother taking care of her child, but I didn't mind.

"I don't think you should have that party tonight," I said, laying him in his bed.

"What? No, no!" he said emphatically. He looked around frantically. "I invited very important nobles here, along with some unimportant ones." He got up and paced back and forth around his bed. "The Marqués de Isla de Arousa is coming! Don't forget the Marqués y Marquesa de Villena. Oh, and the Marqués de Iria Flavia will be here too." He stopped and sat back down, slouched over, and held his horns. "Oh no," he groaned.

"Ronaldo?"

"I invited Duque y Duquesa de Alba as well. Ohh this is not good."

"The Duke? Ronaldo, they'll ruin you if you don't play your cards right."

"I know!" he shouted. "I know. I can't let them see me like this." He threw off his coat and lay down with a loud groan.

It had been a long while since I'd been to a party, which gave me an idea. "Hmm, maybe I can go in your place?" He looked up at me with a raised eyebrow. "I'll be you, and you can be my tired, drunk friend. They don't know what you look like yet."

"You'd do that for me, perrito?"

"Of course, amigo." I nodded. "Besides, it's been a while since I've been able to have some fun."

I went into his closet and looked for an outfit to wear for the party as I heard the bull groaning in bed.

"Perrito," he called. "Can you bring me the basket in the restroom, por favor?" I didn't need to ask what he needed it for as I looked at his green-tinted face. I rushed into the restroom and fetched him the blue wicker basket that was on the floor. He snatched the basket from me, gagging and heaving into it. The smell filled the air and made my stomach turn. I sprung back into the closet to get away from the smell, and looked around for an outfit.

I found a blue silk coat with gold buttons, along with black trousers and matching colored shoes. Lucky for me, he wasn't much larger than I was. I tried on the outfit; it was loose but manageable. I heard the bull snoring, peeked out the closet, and saw him sprawled out on the bed. I chuckled as I fixed my collar in the mirror, then stepped out.

Since I knew my way around the estate, I went downstairs and made ready for the party. I called one of his servants.

"Excuse me," I said. "Ronaldo needs fresh berries and tapas from the marketplace."

"Sí, Señor. Might I ask, where is El Marqués? It's not like him to be late for his own party."

"Ronaldo—he's, oh dear," I replied, "he's sick at the moment. He's in bed now. Let him rest."

"Oh, y-yes, my lord." He went into the living room with some of the other servants, then they grabbed their coats and headed out the door. They seemed to know what they were doing, so I left them alone.

As the servants went shopping, I practiced my speeches and prepared to mingle with the guests. To help myself assume the role of host, I practiced in front of the mirror.

"Buenos días," I said as I bowed my head at my reflection. A bit too formal, I thought. "Buenos días y bienvenidos!" I repeated with more enthusiasm. However, my smile looked too eager. If I wanted to make an impression and help out Ronaldo, I would have to step out of my comfort zone and be more social than I usually was.

I'd also run the risk of someone familiar with Ronaldo encountering me.

A couple of hours later, the servants returned with food, tapas, and wine. One of them had also hired musicians to perform. Hearing Ronaldo upstairs groaning, I went upstairs with a servant to check on him and saw him sitting on his bed.

"Oh, I don't feel so good," he said as he held his head and lay back down. "Even sober, I don't think I'm going to do this party."

"Are you sure?" I asked. "I got everything we need. It'll look quite wonderful. You don't at least want to see it?"

"If I know my workers, I'll take your word, perrito. I promise, I'll repay you. Go on, now; guests will surely arrive soon. I'm going to rest a bit more. Don't have too much fun." He chuckled, shifted onto his side, and pulled the sheets over himself. "Pepe and the others know what to do in a situation like this." He pointed to the servant. "Pepe, I'm counting on you and the others. See to it that things go well."

"Sí, Señor," replied the servant as he nodded and left us.

"Rest well, my friend." I closed the door gently.

I went downstairs and heard a knock on the door. I saw a servant rush past me.

"Perdóneme, Señor," she said as she quickly opened the door. "Welcome, Marquesa." She led the Marquesa into the grand hall and introduced her. "I present to you, my lord, Emilia Rimirez de la Melena Negro."

"A pleasure, Marqués," I said in greeting, taking her silk-gloved hand and kissing it.

"Ohh, the pleasure is mine, Ronaldo," she replied as she put her hand on her cheek and chuckled. "Forgive my ignorance, but many stories have told me that you were a— how one would say," she cleared her throat, "a grotesque brute."

"Ronaldo?" I looked around before remembering my role. "Oh, I-yes! Er, only stories, my lady Emilia." I returned the chuckle. "Hopefully I will prove them wrong today." I gestured toward a long sofa in the living room. "Please."

"Well, you've certainly proved me wrong, my dear," she replied as she sat.

Soon, I heard the door knock and saw another servant rush to the door. "Welcome, my lords and ladies!" He invited six nobles into the estate. "My lord, I present to you, Marqués Ivan de los Jardines de Aranjuez," Ivan stepped forward and held my hand.

"A pleasure, amigo," he said as I gave him a polite nod.

"Duque Ignacio Acosta Rivera-Maradona y Trujillo," the servant continued, "his brother Duque Raul, and his wife Duquesa Valentina de Moctezuma de Tultengo." They bowed to me while Valentina curtseyed.

"And finally, presenting Duque Juan Carlos Manuel Pereria de Toledo and his sister, Ximena Manuela Pereria Colón Gorosábel-Carvajal y Maroto, de Veragua."

As he introduced Ximena, I hid my face under my headwear in hopes that she wouldn't notice my familiar face.

"A pleasure to finally meet you, Señor," said Juan Carlos as he approached me. "Ronaldo, was it?" All I could wonder was how he fit clothes over his antlers.

"Yes, Marques. The pleasure is mine" I replied with a bow.

"It is an honor to meet you. You look… smaller than I remember as a child; different. Then again, we were only old enough to toddle."

"I…um…yes." I fumbled over my words. "T-the years have changed me quite a bit." It was obvious that he knew who Ronaldo was. This meant that I would have to keep him away from the others, as well as keeping my distance from Ximena.

Almost an hour after the party started, the estate was near bursting with partygoers. So far, I had avoided Ximena; however, I lost sight of Juan Carlos. I saw servants rushing and bustling around with tapas in hand and serving food, water, and wine. The musicians played lively music in the ballroom. I went in and saw many guests dancing.

"Care to dance?" someone asked as I felt a poke on my shoulder. I turned around and saw Juan Carlos' smile. "Ronaldo?" My heart beat harder. I didn't know what the deer had been doing or saying to others, but he wore a subtle smirk.

"Two men? Dancing together?" I chuckled. "Is that acceptable? We'd rather not have a riot on our hands, yes?"

"All of the people in here, they're more interested in who would get drunk first. Besides, his—your guards are getting suspicious." His eyes trailed left and right. I subtly glanced up to the guards on the balconies. "It'd be nice for them to see me doing something harmless."

"Very well, I suppose." I nodded. As he held his hand out, I placed my hand on top. We entered the dance floor side-by-side, hand in hand. I led him as we started dancing.

"Interesting, Ronaldo," he said. "Usually I lead us around the dancefloor. Remember in dance class?" We kept dancing as I fell behind, and Juan Carlos started leading.

"Oh, I, uh…yes. Of course, I remember." The deer kept looking down at my feet.

"Hmm, let's stop this charade, amigo." He chuckled, but kept dancing. "You are not Ronaldo. You never have been, and you never will be. While many of these idiots wouldn't be able to tell a door from a wall, I'm not them." He looked back up at me. "Who are you, anyway, wolf?"

Seeing as my cover was blown, there was no reason to hide it anymore. However, I didn't want to ruin Ronaldo's chances of getting in Duque Ignacio or Juan Carlos's good graces.

"What are you going to do now? Get him in trouble?" I asked as we kept dancing. He chuckled and leaned in, lips close to my ear.

"I can keep quiet if you wish," he whispered.

"Really?" I paused for a moment, then continued dancing. "What do you want in return?"

"Hm, there's always a catch. A price." His hand slid down my back, resting right above my bottom. "I could do good things for you and Ronaldo. I am a duke after all. I'm sure a lowly don such as you would like to experience the more luxurious lifestyle among the marquisate, or even a dukedom."

"Joaquín Baldomero Fernández-Espartero y Alvarez de la Patilla; or simply Baldo—wait, how did you know I was a don?" I asked as we kept dancing. I noticed a few of the dancing couples had left the floor.

"It's all over your face, lobo. As for lying, it was a bad deed, but for a good cause. I respect that. However, deception comes with a price. You help me, I'll help you and Ronaldo."

"So, what do you want from me then, Juan Carlos?" I looked up at him seriously. "Ronaldo is my friend. I want to be there for him."

"My lovely wife has been a thorn in my side, deciding that I'm not pleasing enough for her. Yet she will parade herself among the other men around town. It can get quite frustrating. I have been very tense and am in need of relief, if you know what I mean. Do you know what I mean, Baldo?" I shook my head and looked up at him with curiosity. "Sexually, Baldo. I need some form of release. Looking at you, I think you could help with that."

The hand on my back slid lower, feeling over my rear.

"Juan. Juan Carlos, I don't—"

"You don't?" he chuckled and gave a smug grin. "Then what's poking me, then? Why have you been blushing, ever since we started dancing? I think you do, or at least you're thinking about it."

I was speechless as we continued to dance. I looked away. Only two more couples were on the floor.

"What do you say?" he asked me. "What's life without a little fun? Persuasion and duplicity—this is how the game is played, Baldo."

"You'll keep quiet about it?" I asked as he dipped me.

"You have my word as a duke."

I heard applause as the music stopped. We were the last couple on the floor. After we walked out of the ballroom, I paused and took a deep breath, then led him upstairs. I nodded at the guard to let us pass, as the upper floor was off-limits to all except for me and Ronaldo.

I led Juan into the guest room and locked the door behind us. I removed my boots and laid them against the wall, then took Juan's boots and did the same. I sat on the bed, looked around the room, and let out a nervous sigh; I had never had sex with another man before. Juan sat beside me and put his hand on my thigh. I felt a slight tingle through my body as his hand slid along my thigh and toward my crotch.

"You're nervous," he said. I saw concern in his eyes.

"I-I've done this with females before," I replied, "but it's just—"

"Relax. Breathe. Let me lead, lobo."

I nodded as the deer pushed me gently onto the bed and planted kisses on my neck. I took a deep breath and exhaled as he suggested, which seemed to relax me.

"Good, now we're ready to start."

He began to kiss my lips, making them quiver. Instead of lying there like a log, I curled an arm around him and rubbed his back. His hooves made their way to the buttons on my jacket and undid them. I did the same for him as he kissed me deeper. As we kissed, I panted through my nose and gave soft pleasured moans. With both of our jackets off, I felt less restricted.

"There, that's better," Juan Carlos said. "Now we can move around more." He began to unbutton my shirt with one hand and rub at my crotch with the other. We continued removing our clothing, piece by piece, clothes tossed in all directions until we were bare. Our throbbing cocks pressed into each other's abs.

He leaned down to kiss me as I curled my arms around him. My body felt more relaxed. I caught the scent of arousal coming off of him—stronger than when we walked into the room, which excited me even more. He slid his tongue into my maw, making me moan louder.

He thrusted against me and kissed along my neck. I felt his tongue trail down my torso. My body quivered as he licked over it. His tongue soon found its way onto my erect member, which was already throbbing with pre. He began to stroke his own member as his tongue trailed over the length of mine and down to my hole. I spread my legs for him to have easier access to my entrance.

The more he loved on me with his tongue, the more relaxed and comfortable I felt with him. I turned him onto his back. As I climbed on top of him, I murred with pleasure and kissed him deeply, just as he had kissed me. I moved down his body, slid his cock into my maw and started bobbing slowly. I heard him groaning deeply as I sucked. I took more and more of his member into my muzzle. I'd never done anything like this. It felt right. The smell of his arousal and the feel of his muscular physique as I ran my hands along his torso made my member throb even more.

He stopped me and flipped me onto my back again. I felt his member poking at my hole. I tensed up and gave a quiet yelp.

"Just relax, lobo," he told me, and smiled. "Trust me." I replied with a nod.

He proceeded to slide his member into me slowly. I let out a gasp and a moan as I grabbed the bedsheets. I'd never felt this before. The pain mixed with pleasure. I stroked my member and looked up at him. His face looked like he was concerned but pleased as well. I pulled him down to steal another kiss. He began giving rhythmic thrusts, tearing soft moans from me with every movement.

He thrust deeper and deeper, getting closer to my prostate. With each thrust, the pain faded more. I grabbed onto his antlers.

"J-Juan," I called out, gasping as he thrusted harder.

I tightened up as he hit my spot, making my member leak more pre. I wrapped my arms around his neck and my legs around his waist, holding onto him tightly. My member rubbed against his hard abs as I got lost in my lust. My eyes rolled up as I felt his member throb hard inside me. My body felt nothing but pleasure.

After almost thirty minutes, he pulled out of me and lay on his back. He took my arm and had me kneel over his lap. I soon sat back onto his member and began to bounce in his lap. My tongue was lolling out as I felt sweat dripping down my body. I was working Juan up as well; I could feel his member throbbing even harder than before.

"L-Lobo, I'm getting close." He panted as well as I saw his eyes shut. I put my hands on his shoulders and bounced harder. His pre coated my passage, letting me ride him faster. The sounds of my rump slapping on his crotch filled the room; having Juan's cock inside me was better than fucking any woman had ever felt.

Even though I was doing this for Ronaldo, I could not help but enjoy Juan Carlos.

"Baldo, I'm going to—" His words trailed off in a loud groan as he climaxed deep inside me.

Hearing those sounds and feeling his seed inside me sent me over the edge and made me orgasm all over his chest and stomach. I let out a loud moan and tilted my head back as I panted heavily. My body was weak from my climax, and I collapsed on top of him. I rested my head on his shoulder. As we recovered, we licked each other clean like feral cats taking a bath. I felt his hoof rubbing my back and looked into his eyes. Those beautiful shades of brown captivated me. I leaned in for a kiss, though he turned away.

"What's wrong, Juan?" I asked as I tilted my head.

"I… you shouldn't get used to this, Baldo," he replied, followed with a sigh. "I have a wife, no? This is, after all, just business; part of the game, if you remember."

I lifted myself off him and sat next to him on the bed, looking away.

"R-right—part of the game," I replied, trying not to sound too disappointed. Juan got off the bed, gathered his clothes, and started dressing.

I sat with my legs crossed. He headed toward the door.

"Baldo?" he called. I turned my head to look at him as my ears perked up. "Thank you."

"For what?" I replied.

"For…inviting me to this exquisite party. You'll surely make an impression." Even though I was expecting something else, hearing him say that still made me smile.

"Enjoy the rest of the party, Juan," I said with a chuckle. He closed the door behind him and I gave a sad and exhausted sigh. I wanted to see him again, but he was right; he had a wife. Who was I to disrupt that? Perhaps exciting things like that— or exciting people like him—only come once in a while.

After getting dressed, I left the room to see that the party had ended. The only people left were the servants. I went into Ronaldo's room to see he remained asleep. I didn't want to wake him, so I went downstairs.

"Ronaldo is still sleeping; let him rest," I told a servant who was cleaning up. I headed toward the front door.

"I hope you enjoyed your stay, Señor?" he asked. I turned around and simply gave him a small chuckle and a smile, then walked out the front door. "Take care," he said behind me.

A few days after the party, I received a letter from the Duchess of Veragua, Ximena.

Hello, Joaquin Baldomero. I'm not sure if you remember me. You might remember my brother, Duque Juan Carlos. He was quite fascinated with you for some reason. He couldn't stop talking about you when we got home. I had no idea you were even there. You must visit our estate someday. Brother said he wishes to continue his game, whatever that means. Do write back, though. I miss our chats over wine. I look forward to having another debate, mi amigo. Until next time, my dear. Duty calls.

Truly yours, Ximena.

I would be crazy to pass up a discussion with the drunk Ximena. Although, it seemed that the best impression I left was on Juan himself. I wrote a letter to Ronaldo, thanking him for letting me take part in this playing field. It would seem the game of nobility had a new player, and his name was Joaquin Baldomero.

Unnatural
South Dakota, United States - 1886 CE

"It's our time, Sam," said the scholar as he walked me through the town, the morning sun sitting in the sky. "They don't have a shred of modernity!" He clenched a fist. "Seeing where they come from, I could tell they were suffering." The Doberman's ears twitched.

"Suffering? How, Mr. William?"

"Did you not just hear me? No schools, no decent clothes. It's tragic, I tell you!" He held his head and sobbed as people began to stare. "It's horrible!"

"Don't you think you're being a bit dramatic, sir?" I bought a red apple from a vendor's cart and continued walking with him.

"Perhaps." He took a bite of the apple that was supposed to be mine. "However, there needs to be some culture in the Da'qite tribe! They need to be saved!

"You mean assimilated?" I raised an eyebrow at him.

"Of course, Samuel, my boy! A little learning of one's culture wouldn't hurt anyone, right? That's why I stayed with them for a month."

As we reached the outskirts of town, I saw three figures approaching from afar, crossing a bridge. I straightened my blue buttoned tunic and jacket.

"And this is where I take my leave, my boy." Hearing that caught me off-guard.

"Wait, what? You're not going to help? But what am—" I saw he was already headed back into the town.

"I know you'll do fine, my little retriever!" he responded, disappearing into a crowd of townsfolk.

As I turned back around, a tall, toned horse with a tribal mask looked down at me. I was stunned by his height. His clothes were close to what I had imagined—a sleeveless loose-fitting shirt tucked into trousers tied with a rope—quite primitive. The shirt showed off his powerful arms. His red, rectangular mask looked as if it was yelling and angry. I realized I should not be staring.

"Welcome to Watertown," I greeted him, waving. "I'm Samuel, but everyone just calls me Sam, or Little Sam. I work at the university with…" I had no idea if he understood anything I said, if he was smiling or frowning beneath that mask, or if he was even paying attention. "I'll be helping you adjust to our lifestyle while you're here." I gave a nervous chuckle. It was as if those giant green-bordered eyes of the mask were staring into my soul. "Well, again, welcome to Sou—"

He hugged me suddenly, as though he had not seen me in ages. His hold was strong, lifting me off the ground and squeezing my back.

"Can't…breathe…" I managed to say. He must have understood that, since he let go of me. I noticed that the other two he arrived with were gone. "You're quite the strong one. I guess you do a lot of physical work?"

He leaned against me and his legs wobbled. He whispered something in a deep voice, but it wasn't in English.

"What's wrong? Are you alright?" I asked, trying to help him up. Soon he became heavier as he fainted. "Hey!" I moved so he would not land on top of me, though he still knocked me down. During the fall, his wooden mask had broken off. "Are you okay?" I turned him over and saw his face, the red circles around his eyes, and three red stripes on each cheek to compliment his dark brown fur. He was a handsome one. Then I remembered he was unconscious.

"Hello? Other tribe friends?" I looked around but saw nobody. "I have to carry you home, don't I?" I sighed and whined. "Why did I have to get the big, strong one?"

I hoisted him over my shoulder and started walking back into town. I heard others chattering as though I was carrying a corpse. "What's he doing? Is that another tribesman? Is he okay?" I made it halfway to my home before one of the townsfolk—a German Shepherd—offered to help me; I was more than thankful, since he took most of the weight.

Arriving at my house, the Shepherd went his own way and left me with the horse. I walked him upstairs into my room and laid him in my bed. Sitting in a chair next to him as he slept, I heard him snore, and I watched him sleep with his mouth open. He was not as handsome when asleep, but amusing to look at. I then heard his stomach growling. Perhaps he didn't have anything to eat or drink, which made him pass out. Perhaps it was the long walk in general.

I noticed a book on my desk that Mr. William had left me. A dictionary. He had made his own dictionary for this tribe. Truly a dedicated man. I started reading it. *What was that word he said? Let's see...* I found the word meaning "fear." Perhaps he had never seen buildings like ours. Mr. William did say that they lived in teepees in the forests. Maybe I was talking too much English and overwhelmed him. No matter the reason, he was a visitor here to learn, and I was his guide.

I turned around and saw him awake, glancing at the desk, wardrobe, and the lamps. I gave a nervous smile and sat down next to him.

"I'm sorry for startling you earlier," I said as he reached out to me. I laid his hand on his chest. "You need your rest. That was a hard fall you took." He simply looked up at me with his stoic brown eyes. He looked calm. "Let me start over." I smiled and placed my hand on my chest. "I'm Samuel." I put my hand on my chest again and talked slower. "Samuel." Perhaps he didn't want to understand or talk to me. "I guess this will be more difficult than I hoped."

I heard his stomach growl again. "You must be hungry. I'll fix you something to eat." I went into the kitchen to fix a vegetable stew for him. Using two brown cloths to protect my hands, I took the pot off the fire and put it on the table. As I turned around, I bumped into the horse. "Hey!" I cried out. "Don't startle me like that. Though, it's good to know you're feeling better."

As I picked up two bowls next to the fire, I heard a pained grunt. I turned my head and saw the horse touch the pot.

"Are you crazy?" I rushed him over to the washstand to cool off his hands. "You should be more careful! At least you weren't burned, though."

I fixed him and myself bowls of stew and pulled out a chair for him. As he looked at me, I nodded at him and smiled, sitting down. As I started eating with my spoon, he joined me, mimicking what I did. *I suppose that's one way of learning.*

I took him into the bathroom afterward to let him relieve himself. The toilet scared him when he heard it flush. I was just glad he did use it and didn't go into a bush.

After we got dressed, the horse wearing what he had before, we left the house and made our way to the university. On the walk there, he stayed behind but very close to me, almost knocking me over twice. The silence from him was almost tiring. At the entrance, the horse looked at the large building, petrified. I put my hand on his shoulder, and we entered together. We found Mr. William conversing with a friend of mine, Alisa.

"Ah, Sam!" he greeted me. and patted my shoulder. "How are things, my boy? Have you been getting acquainted with Qintola?"

"Qintola? Oh, yes!" I chuckled, finally learning the horse's name. "In a way, I suppose. I don't think he ate all day, so I fixed him a meal." I shrugged and scratched behind my ear.

"Let's talk," said the scholar. "Alisa, be a dear and show our friend around while I talk with Sam." Alisa led Qintola away from us into another room, leaving Mr. William and I alone. "Has he talked to you yet?"

"The only thing he said to me was 'fear'." I sighed and shook my head, leaning against a desk. "I don't think I'm capable of this task. I don't even think he likes me."

"Well, did you allow him to greet you?" He crossed his arms, and I nodded. "Did you let him do the secondary greeting? When meeting someone for the first time, the Da'qite hug them first. Their second greeting is the stroking of the cheek and nodding, to show respect to the acquaintance."

I threw my hands up and scoffed. "Wouldn't that be something you should have told me before I met him? I had to carry his unconscious body all the way to my house after he fainted!" I gasped as I remembered this morning. "Oh, I'm a fool. I stopped him from doing the second greeting. Maybe he does hate me. I hope I didn't ruin this for him."

"Or me!" shouted Mr. William. "I'm the one who told the chairman that this was a good idea."

"It's not about just you!" I argued.

Alisa and Qintola returned, the horse looking nervous; did he hear our argument?

"Go home, you two," said the scholar as he waved at Qintola and me. "We'll talk tomorrow. And I'll see Qintola in class for his English lesson."

As Qintola and I walked back to my home, it began to drizzle rain, and we rushed the rest of the way. Only a little wet from the rain, I shook off the excess water. Then I looked at the horse. I thought about what Mr. William said. I had never allowed Qintola to perform his second greeting with me.

"Qintola?" I stood in front of him, looking into his stoic eyes. I hesitated but then figured, *what do I have to lose?* I stroked his cheek with my hand and nodded. He looked at me with a surprised expression as I smiled. He stroked my own cheek and smiled back to me.

"Sam...Samuel?" he finally said with his deep voice.

"That's right," I responded, nodding. I was happy that I hadn't ruined this opportunity. Even though he didn't "trust" me, he trusted me when going to the university. Or perhaps I was the only person he knew. That didn't matter, right now.

What did matter was, with him learning English and willing to talk to me, it would be easier for me to teach him about our culture.

I was running out of potatoes and vegetables, however, and had to get more. This was the perfect time for me to test Mr. William's dictionary.

"I have to go for a little while." I looked at the book and tried to translate what I had said. However, the horse looked at me as though I had grown another head. I searched for something easier to communicate. "Stay here," I commanded in his language as I put my hand out. He nodded and sat down. I sighed with relief and left the house. I could not help feeling like a pet owner, commanding and training Qintola.

At the farmer's store I picked out two bags of potatoes and three bags of vegetables. When I got home, Qintola hugged me as if I had been gone for a week. I belatedly realized that as it was only the first day he had been here, I should have been more considerate than to leave him here alone.

That night, I laid out a makeshift bed with a spare sheet and spread in the room across the hall for him. "This is where you sleep, okay?" Exhausted, I went into my room and took off my shirt, and changed into my night trousers. "Goodnight, Qintola. Hopefully we have a better tomorrow." I blew out the candle, exhaled, and closed my eyes.

The next morning, I felt myself cuddling something soft and warm. I opened my eyes and realized I was cuddling Qintola, who was in cloth undergarments. I gasped as he held me close to him, hearing him snort. He seemed asleep. He felt so good! I was only supposed to help him learn, not do…this. At least nobody could see. I'd rather people not think I was some devil or being corrupted.

"Hey! Let go!" I pushed him away, and he fell out of the bed. as the horse woke up and rubbed his eyes. "This isn't your bed, Qintola!" He just looked at me with those calm eyes, almost sadly. He said another word in his language: *Nivgaw'as.* "Wait, wait." I picked up the dictionary and flipped through the pages. The word translated to "natural." "This is natural in your tribe? Well, here that is..." I searched for unnatural. "Nivgaw'asan. I don't want people getting the wrong idea. We'd both be in trouble then."

Hearing that, the horse looked down in disappointment. He then looked at me with those handsome brown eyes. "Would you...stop it with the face? A big guy like you shouldn't be making faces like that." I put the book down and crossed my arms, looking out the window at townsfolk walking about and chatting.

"Well, you have quite the day ahead of you. Need to get washed up and dressed. I'll go and get—where did you go?" I looked around the room, but he was nowhere to be seen. For a big horse, he knew how to move quietly. "Qintola?" I searched the house, but to no avail. I threw on a shirt, robe, and shoes, and headed outside. With the sun barely over the horizon, he could not have gotten far. "Qintola?" I called again.

"Hey, Sam," called a fruit cart vendor. "You're taking care of one of those dirty tribesmen, right?"

"What did you call him?" I approached the man with a growl.

"Easy, lad." The pig put his hands up and snorted. "I saw him heading out of town. Maybe he couldn't handle having some culture. Good riddance, I'd say."

I wanted to respond, but I had no time to argue. I headed outside town, making my way to the bridge where I had met the horse. I saw a few pups watching, pointing, and giggling at something. The tribesman was bathing in the river next to the bridge.

"Samuel!" he called with a smile on his face.

"How did you...you don't..." At the risk of soaking my clothes, I went into the river and pulled him out "Come on!" As he followed me out of the water, the pups gasped. "What?" I yelped in surprise when I realized the horse was completely naked. I stood in front of him to cover his private parts. "Okay, kids. Nothing to see here." I chuckled nervously and gestured to them to leave. "Run along now."

After they left, I groaned. "Here. Put this on." I handed him my robe; it only reached his knees, but covered his groin at least. He said 'natural'. "I know. It is for you, but you're here to learn and…possibly assimilate."

Hearing that word made his eyes open wide, as though it brought up memories. His eyebrows furrowed and his teeth clenched. He shouted words in his language.

"Sure, that." I nodded agreeably. "Come on. We need to get you cleaned up and dressed."

Going back through the town, we walked by the fruit vendor. He scoffed at Qintola while he wiped down his cart. He kept his eyes on the horse the whole time, looking like they were going to pop out of his head. Again, I wanted to argue with the ignorant man, but didn't have time.

Others looked at Qintola as well, either with disgust, infatuation, or curiosity. Whether it was because he was a tribesman or that he wore nothing but a small robe, it didn't matter; we were drawing attention—which could be a good or bad thing.

Back at home, I bathed the horse. Scrubbing him down with soap and water in the tub, he made sure I reached every inch of him; I supposed the Da'qite were strict about cleanliness (in their own terms). I gave him back his clothes and tied his black hair in a ponytail. After we ate breakfast, we went to the university, where Mr. William was waiting eagerly to bombard Qintola with his teachings.

"Welcome back, my boys!" he bellowed with his tail wagging. "Qintola…" he greeted him just as Qintola had greeted me. They started talking in Qintola's native tongue, and the horse smiled. Mr. William gestured to his classroom, and the horse went in. The classrooms were able to fit 20 students each, but the horse was the only student in his class.

"It must be refreshing for him to hear his native tongue." I peeked into the small room to see the tribesman sitting at a desk.

"Just you wait." The scholar crossed his arms and grinned. "When I'm done with him, you won't even remember English isn't his first language." He let out a guffaw and headed into the classroom, closing the door. While I was worried about how Qintola's first class would turn out, I knew that he was in good hands. Mr. William might have come on strong, but he was an expert linguist and mentor.

I worked on my own studies in the library. I looked at the others working and reading. While trying to focus on my work, I couldn't take my mind off Qintola's studies. I remembered Mr. William's remark about Qintola's people being intelligent, though. A tap on my shoulder startled me. I turned around and saw Alisa smiling at me.

"Hello, Sam. Mind if I sit?" I couldn't refuse the cute puppy dog face she made as the fur on her cheeks poofed out, looking innocent. She sat down in front of me and placed her books on the table. I looked blankly at the table. "I know that look. What's wrong?"

"Sometimes, I wonder if I'm cut out for doing this," I replied, shaking my head. "He's learning about our culture, but I don't know the first thing about his. The only thing I learned is that they sleep together and they greet each other differently."

"You've taken this field of study for a reason, right? To learn about the lifestyles of other cultures." She smiled and opened her history book, showing me pictures of different tribes and people.

"What if he doesn't want to assimilate?" I looked at the pictures. "He lashed out at me when I mentioned it." I sighed. "Though, I can't blame him. I'm sure their culture is very important to them. To take that away from them…"

"He can still learn about ours, Sam." She smiled at me. "Who said he has to give up his own? Just like how you can learn about his without leaving yours behind."

I nodded and smiled. "I understand now. Thank you, Alisa."

After his studies, I waited for Qintola outside the building. He left with books and papers, putting them in a black bag.

"I hope studying went well?" I asked, looking up at him, but he gave no response. "I see Mr. William gave you some books to read? That was nice of him." Perhaps he didn't understand me yet.

Not much talking was done on the way home. When we got there, he quickly sat at the table and opened his books. I looked over, and saw writing in them already.

"Well, you do have remarkable penmanship." I sat next to him, drinking a cup of water.

"H-hello…Samuel," he said as he looked at me. "I…am Qintola." Hearing him work through that made me smile.

"Good job, Qintola." I nodded to him and looked at his books.

"Samuel is…friend?"

"Yes. I am your friend." I smiled. He then took my hand and held it. Perhaps it was another custom of his.

As his studies continued, his language skills improved. I improved my linguistic skills as well, so I could better understand his native tongue.

After his class, a few women crowded the area next to the university entrance; they giggled, their dresses swaying as the tall horse stood over them, unfazed by their constant attention. Once he saw me, he walked over, wearing the same calm look he usually gave. I smiled as we headed home.

"You know, Qintola, there's no harm in going out and having a good time with people. I know studying helps, but too much studying hurts."

"I like studying," he responded. "I like Samuel." He caressed my cheek as he had when we met. Perhaps that was a symbol for friendship. I returned the gesture and smiled.

"I'm sure you'd have more fun spending time with people other than this boring dog every day."

He stayed silent and looked at me, calm as usual. When we reached my home, he returned to his studying and writing.

As we got ready to go to sleep, I said goodnight to Qintola and blew out the candle on the bedstand, but left the door open, my room next to his. Knowing that he was improving and learning at a steady pace, I was grateful to have Mr. William help him learn English. I regretted this task less and less.

The next day, a crash of thunder woke me up. Once again, I felt a horse holding me in his arms.

"Qintola," I looked over at him, seeing that he was already awake, "what did we talk about before?" As lightning flashed and thunder boomed, he shut his eyes and held me tighter. Since sleeping alone was not his nature, sleeping alone during a storm must have been terrifying. "I'm sorry. I should have known." I rubbed his cheek and let him hold me. "Though, I guess it is time to get ready for the day."

I fixed some eggs for him, but he had his head in his books, writing and reading.

"You should at least eat, Qintola." I moved his books out the way so I could set his plate down. "You might not eat first in your tribe, but here, we eat to stay energized."

As we ate, a softer thunderclap boomed, scaring the horse. Perhaps his tribe always travelled together instead of alone.

After the storm passed, I decided to take Qintola shopping, in order to get some fresh air. I brought a large blanket for a picnic after we went shopping as we went into the town, getting interested looks as we had before. As we went into a clothing store, I saw the fruit vendor from earlier, snorting as he looked at different shirts. He spotted us as well and approached us, his stench getting stronger, leading Qintola to hold his nose.

"Well, well," he said, his belly jiggling as he walked. "Look at what we have here."

"We don't want any trouble, friend," I replied.

"Well you got it! And I'm not your friend, dog, and I'm certainly not his damn friend." He pushed on the horse with his belly. "Damn horses. Thinking you can just come here without even a how-do-you-do, just a bunch of rapists and wild braying beasts." While his accusations were partially true from what I've studied, I did not want to give him the satisfaction.

"Now, hold on just a minute!" I stood in front of Qintola. "Qintola isn't doing any of that, not that it's any of your business. He's learning about our culture. He is under mine and Scholar William's care. If you have a problem with Qintola, you'll have to go through me, you hear?" I pushed him back.

The pig furrowed his eyebrows and groaned. "You're a lucky horse. But your pup won't always be around." He left the store, grumbling to himself.

"Sorry you had to see that." I looked up to the horse, seeing a worried look on his face. "Don't worry, Qintola. You're a guest in this town, and you're my friend. There are people like him in our town, I'll admit, but I won't let anything happen to you."

"Thank you, Samuel." He put his hand on my shoulder. I nodded in response and smiled. "You fought him…for me."

"Well, I wouldn't say I fought him." I chuckled and blushed. "You're my friend, Qintola. Come on; let's see if we can get you something nice-looking."

As we picked out a white buttoned shirt, brown pants, and a brown jacket to try, he tugged at the outfit, as though he felt confined or smothered. I unbuttoned the top button of his shirt, even though there was more than enough room to breathe. Perhaps he didn't like the clothes that we wore. Instead I let him pick out what he wanted: a shirt and trousers similar to what he was already wearing.

"It looks great on you, Qintola."

After we paid and left, the horse started sniffing the air, and hummed with curiosity as he focused on a sweets shop.

"Oh, you want some sweets?" I asked. He nodded and licked his lips. "Let's go, then. If you like the smell, you will love the taste." I grinned as we headed to the shop. The smell became stronger and clearly more intoxicating to Qintola, as if he's never had anything like sugar-filled foods in his tribe. Perhaps he hasn't. As we ordered a bag of fudge, the horse looked eager to dig in. I took the bag and we left, and he immediately tried to take it from me.

"Relax; we want to keep the fudge nice and warm. Trust me—they'll be more enjoyable that way." I chuckled at how eager he was, even though the sweet aroma enticed me as well.

Walking to a nearby lake outside of town, I laid the blanket I'd brought on some grass, then we sat down and I gave him the bag of fudge. He scarfed them down as though he had never eaten before. He caught himself, however, and offered me a few. I happily accepted, and enjoyed the sugary goodness. He soon attempted to make light conversation.

"The water at the lake…like home." He pointed to the crystal blue water reflecting the sunlight.

"You lived near a lake, too? It must've been nice to be in tune with nature."

"Nature, yes." He looked at a crow flying and cawing. "Your world. Little nature here. Only big houses and buildings. It is…different. Unnatural."

"I suppose it would be." I looked away, thinking about the differences our cultures had. "Perhaps I do have more to learn than just the language." I listened to the cawing and the other wildlife beyond the river.

"Study. Like me. Together." He put his head on my shoulder. "I will help you. Like you."

"Thank you, Qintola. I appreciate that." Was this another gesture of friendship? I patted his head and smiled.

For some reason, that moment made me feel closer to him, like a barrier between us had been destroyed. Maybe it was the English lessons, or maybe it was what he said. Whatever it was, I was glad to be the one chosen for the scholar's mission, and I'm glad Qintola was the person who I got to teach.

Your Feet
Marseille, France - 1918 CE

"Your feet," said André as he pointed his sabre at his pupil's bare feet.

"What?" Léon asked with a confused look on his face. He looked down at his bay-colored feet and curled his toes. "What about them?"

The senior lion chuckled under his breath, and rotated his foil in a circle twice before sheathing it, swiftly and elegantly. His keen green eyes measured the ability of his adept, who was holding his en garde position against him.

"Your feet, you don't move them nearly enough. You treat the foil as your weapon, while it is nothing but the tip that you should be attacking with. Your entire body and the potential to anticipate any number of at least ten moves ahead via being in a constant motion."

That did the trick, as the younger lion let out a roar and lunged against his senior trainer. The older peer was quicker, however, as he already unsheathed his blade. With a simple dodge, the teacher pointed the sharp edge of his weapon at the back of the trainee's neck.

"Touché, boy."

The young one folded his ears down in defeat, wiping some sweat off his forehead, until his master pulled the sword away. The 18th century fencing style was one of the most elegant that he knew, and his trainer had time and again demonstrated the capacity to humiliate him.

Without a single moment of rest, the older feline assumed his en garde position and motioned with his left hand for his student to try another lunge.

"Position one. Go."

The lower left part of the torso of a right-handed duelist, more specifically, where he drew the sword from—that was the particular target his trainer was asking for him to assault. A strike to the leg would incapacitate his opponent, preventing them from fighting again.

"And this time, anticipate the gu—" he said, as Léon interrupted with another thrust of his foil.

Perhaps he lunged in before fully appreciating that last piece of information; the young adult wasn't entirely sure. In an instant, his master had not only parried his attempt at an attack, but, turning around on his agile hind-paws while extending his arm, also managed to twist his grasp around his good right arm, keeping the sharp foil away from him and threatening the student again, the blade once more touching his throat.

"I was going to say anticipate the guard. Did you do that?" The elder lion asked with a stoic look and furrowed brows, as Léon shook his head.

With that, and a loud grunt, André pulled on the student's left arm, dragging the younger lion off balance and a few feet across the room, and most importantly, out of harm's way.

"Position one. Again." André demanded as he held his blade upward.

Léon decided to take it easy this time. *Try to anticipate the defense*, he thought to himself, taking a deep breath and relaxing. A pass, delicately, of the preparation foot past the lunging one. Then, while getting in reach, a good thrust against his master's lower torso.

Yet again, however, Léon had to face a trick that made his teacher one of the most revered duelists in the land. The older lion, who always wore a thick leather glove on his balancing hand, the left one, used said apparel against his own blade to parry and rotate the foil of his student. Pushing back, and then simply lashing out his blade, he pointed it right against Léon's groin. Another threat, another lesson, and yet another win.

"Session's over, Léon. Time for some theory."

With that, he withdrew his sword and turned around, taking off his white shirt and using the fabric to wipe sweat off of his well-shaped muscular frame, before throwing it to the side along with his foil.

The younger felid took off his own shirt. Both of them bare-chested, sweaty, and tired, Léon couldn't help but stare at André's glistening, taut body and his sparkling green eyes. Léon's lustful eyes trailed lower, until he noticed his older companion's left leg. It was quivering uncontrollably. His eyes turned from lustful to concerned.

"You...your leg," said the worried kitten.

"What?"

He pointed his foil at the quaking limb. André had injured his leg in three places while he was in the First Army during World War I. His unit was stationed in and around the commune of Carency. He and some of his close friends had been freerunning along some rooftops, most likely showing off their parkour skills. His footpaw missed a ledge, which resulted in him taking a nasty fall. Luckily for him, it was only a two-story building. He was discharged soon after. He'd never been the same since that incident.

"Oh, it's fine. It's probably just the exertion. That was quite the session we had."

His smile was telling the pupil not to worry, but his slowly drooping ears were filling Léon with concern. He stepped closer to André, offering a hand. His older companion refused it, and started wiping the sweat from his face. Soon after, his injured leg started trembling more. Léon noticed the trembling getting fiercer—by now both of André's legs were wobbling.

"André?"

The older lion nearly collapsed, groaning in pain. Léon quickly rushed over and held him up.

"You okay? Easy now..."

He set the big felid down gently, and leaned him against the wall. Léon started massaging his injured leg with one broad hand, stroking his mane with the other.

"I'm not as young as I used to be. I suppose I should remember that, hm?"

They both chuckled softly. André had raised Léon as though he was his own. Never had the older felid felt closer to anyone in his life, and neither had the younger. Léon gazed at his senior's emerald eyes, while André stared back into his own golden eyes. Léon leaned in toward the broad senior lion.

"Léon, I..." André slowly, reluctantly stopped his fast student. Léon's ears drooped, and his face turned dark red.

"I-I'm sorry... are you okay?" asked the embarrassed student, as he looked away in shame. "How's your leg?" He inspected the upper thigh of the older felid's right leg. Léon started to feel around, to find out where André was hurting the most. As he felt immediately above André's knee, his senior winced softly. "Right there?"

"Y-yeah..." André replied with a chuckle, though he also flinched. "I need to remember this leg is not as strong as it used to be..." The elder's ears drooped in shame. "I'm sorry you have to see your teacher like this." He lowered his head, placing his right hand on the back of it.

"Hey..." Léon lifted his teacher's chin and smiled at him softly. "It's not your fault. You're doing what you have to, André." He pressed his smaller nose against the older feline's. "I guess we should cut this session short?" he asked while offering his small brown hand. The older lion took his hand and slowly stood up. "Easy there... Do you need any help getting home?" The student let André lean against him.

"I'd enjoy the company..." the elder said as he nodded. Léon let the other lion lean against him as they walked to his home. "And it seems like you've gotten stronger?" André felt the firmness of the young one's upper arm.

"Oh...well, I've been making more time to exercise," he replied, flexing playfully, but blushing as well. "I'm... trying to keep up with you..." He blushed even more and looked away, trying to hide it.

"I'll say. You tired me out today, child. Not something that usually happens," André replied with a chuckle.

Léon had never been this close to his master. He could barely contain his excitement, trying to hide his wide smile. They passed by the sparkling water of Somme River near his house. When they finally made it to André's house, it was nightfall. He gently laid the elder on his couch. "I'd...better get going. It's getting late for me..." Léon didn't like the dark, despite being a *strong* lion, even as a cub. Even so, he had to go home if he was uninvited to stay.

"There's nothing wrong with staying here for the night, is there?" André sat up on the couch, patting the seat next to him. "Like I said, I'd enjoy the company." He smiled. Léon complied and nervously sat next to the larger lion. He blushed once more.

"Th-thank you for letting me stay here, André. I appreciate it." He smiled softly and held the bigger lion's broad golden hand. His nerves made him shiver.

"It's ok, Léon. No need to be nervous." André pulled the younger lion into his strong arms for a warm embrace. Léon nuzzled deeply into André's soft chest tuft. The older lion felt something poke his thigh. "Er...Léon...?"

The young, embarrassed lion quickly sat up, at a loss for words. "I..."

"It's ok." André rubbed the smaller lion's chest and stomach. "I'd be lying if I said I wasn't a bit... excited." He chuckled and revealed the tent in his pants. Léon face turned a bright red, seeing André's concealed erection. The big felid's broad hand dragged a finger down Léon's chest and over the tent that the kitten had in his trousers. "I'm going to clean up. Make yourself comfortable, okay?"

"Are you... sure you don't need any help washing?" Léon asked nervously, helping up the recovering older lion. André nodded and grinned at the young timid felid, as they walked over to the bathroom.

Léon turned on the water, then helped André undress and settle into the tub. The younger lion couldn't help but stare, amazed by the elder lion's muscled physique. He laid André's clothes out on a table.

"Well?" asked the elder lion. Léon's ears perked up in confusion. "You don't want to get your clothes wet while you're in here, hmm?" Léon nodded and quickly stripped down, laying his clothes next to André's. He slowly got into the tub, being careful of André's leg. He gave a soft, relieving sigh, feeling the warm water on his fur.

The senior lion moved in toward the young one, neither of them able to contain their raging erections any longer. André grabbed his friend's hard-on and started stroking it slowly, causing Léon to start moaning softly. He then saw André's hand on both of their members, picking up the pace as he stroked them.

Léon halted the bigger lion, climbing on top of him for a kiss. He then curled a hand around André's cock, prodding his tail hole with the older lion's larger lionhood.

"Are you sure about this, Léon?" he asked with concern in his emerald eyes. "I...I don't want to hurt you..." He looked into the young lion's eyes and caught a glimpse of his own brutal past.

"Y-yeah, I'm sure. That was long ago. I trust you, André," the cub replied softly, and nodded.

He slowly sat down on André, gasping softly as the elder felid's member slipped inside of his tight hole.

"You ok?" André asked with a concerned look on his face. Léon nodded again. "We'll take it slow and gentle, alright?" He tried to comfort the young felid, softly rubbing his legs. "Let me know if it hurts..."

Léon continued to sit on his teacher's larger member, relaxing a bit, getting used to the feel of it. The young lion couldn't help but run his hands over André's glistening torso, and leaned down to plant a soft kiss on his maw. Feeling more comfortable, Léon started to move up and down slowly, and started moaning quietly from the sensations. Seeing the young one becoming more relaxed with him, André thrusted into him—the younger lion's small but toned physique arousing him further. Neither of them had felt this close with anyone before. Having enough space to move around in the tub, André turned Léon on his back and took the lead by thrusting even harder. This time, Léon felt nothing but pure pleasure and ecstasy. The larger lion grabbed the younger's hands, and they locked claws together. Letting go of each other's hands, Léon's sensual moans complemented André's groans and grunts. Léon's balls tingled as his teacher started massaging them lightly, increasing the sensation even more.

"Oh...André..." he moaned with his eyes shut and his mouth wide open. His panting became more rapid, his body clenching around André's member tightly and gripping his hands. As he started leaking pre on his stomach, the elder felid stroked his pre covered cock and thrusted even deeper and harder. Their moans and groans grew louder still.

André pulled out shortly after, and started stroking both of their members in one hand, his other pinning the student's smaller hands. He leaned down for a deep kiss, slipping his long feline tongue into Léon's maw—Léon's own tongue slipping into the elder lion's mouth. Moaning into the kiss, Léon and André's members both started throbbing and swelling. Their erotic panting became even louder...

"Oh gods, Léon...!" André released waves of his spunk all over Léon and himself, thrusting wildly and groaning heavily. Léon gasped in ecstasy, feeling some of his senior's seed hit his face.

"A-André... I can't... I can't hold it in anymore..." Moments after he said that, Léon shot out ropes of his own cum on their chests. Léon's member throbbed against André's as he shot more streams of his feline juice all over their bodies. The larger lion collapsed on top of the smaller, Léon enjoying his body being pressed beneath André's. "Wow..." he said, both of them panting heavily. The young lion wrapped his arms around André's neck and pulled him down for a kiss.

"You were... amazing, Léon," André replied, making the student's cheeks turn scarlet. André looked into Léon's golden eyes and kissed him once again. "Now, what's say we take a proper bath, before our fur is stained? You know, one that isn't filled with..." He trailed off, chuckled softly, and then stood up, helping Léon up as well. He led Léon to the river.

Léon licked André's spunk off his face, as the elder lion did the same. He pulled Léon under the lukewarm water, rubbing across his back and holding him close. As both of them began growing erect once more, Léon went for broke... "Do you, er... want to go again?" His ears went down in embarrassment, and his cheeks turned rosy once more.

André's ears, however, perked up in surprise. "You sure, Léon?" he asked, looking down at the shy yet eager lion. Noticing the young one's soft smile and throbbing arousal, he brushed his broad hand down Léon's wet mane and pressed their muzzles together for a sweet, passionate kiss. The experienced lion pressed his body against his student's, their members pulsing against each other. Léon turned around, rubbing his rump against André's swollen member, as André ran his hands along Léon's shining, wet torso. "You've such a nice body, Léon..."

He placed his hand on the back of André's head, gently pressing their foreheads together, and leaning the older lion against the edge of the river. He gyrated even harder against the big lion's crotch. André started to purr deeply and pulled Léon's hips closer. André started teasing the young feline's hole with his member, as Léon started moaning once again. The older lion then slid his length inside of Léon, a bit quicker this time, and began thrusting deeply into the young lion.

"F-fuck, André..." Léon closed his eyes, feeling the pleasure of André thrusting inside of him again. The teacher closed his eyes as well, plunging deeper inside his student. Léon's moans grew louder with each thrust. André stroked Léon's shaft as he picked up his pace. Léon bent over, taking the expert's length deeply and hotly.

"Ohh... Léon. Tu es merveilleux." André bent over his student, suckling on his neck and licking his upper back. He softly pulled on the young lion's mane as his thrusts became more intense. Soon he started leaking pre inside him. "Oh, Léon... I'm getting close..." He gripped Léon's hips tightly, claws grazing them. Léon started growling softly as André's hand moved over him more rapidly.

"I'm getting close again, André..." He growled louder and started leaking pre over André's hand, putting his hands on the edges of the river. He continued moaning with pleasure, unconsciously thrusting as well. With each thrust, he gave a loud roar as he started shooting his seed all over the river. At the same time, André released torrents of cum inside of Léon and released a bellowing roar of his own. "F-fuck, André!" They both panted heavily as André pulled out. The strong teacher winced as his bad leg buckled.

"Take it easy..." Léon said with concern as he helped André stand. He drenched the big feline with water, reaching around him, and washing the fur on his back. He slowly sat André down to rest his leg and kept washing him carefully.

"You're such an amazing lion," the student said unconsciously.

"Léon..." André said softly. "Would you like to sleep with me tonight?" His ears drooped in embarrassment from his words. Léon's ears perked up, however. He looked down at André, nodded, and gave a warm smile.

"I'd love to, André."

With them completely clean, the young lion carefully helped the elder out of the river. André led Léon back to his home and helped him dry off. They went into his bedroom and Léon sat on the bed.

"I...should mention. I don't wear anything when I sleep," Léon said with a bright red face. "I... hope that's ok with you?"

"After what we just did? And twice, as I recall. I would encourage it," the older lion replied with a playful smirk. He sat on the bed, next to the young one. They both lay next to each other, and Léon laid his head on the big lion's chest tuft. André held the small lion close to him and started purring, enjoying the intimacy between them. Thinking about what Léon might say if he shared his true feelings, he shed a small tear, and nuzzled the young lion's head. The exhausted Léon started to doze off.

André slowly sat up on the edge of the bed, not waking Léon. He sighed softly and his ears drooped again. "I wish...I could tell you, Léon..." he said to himself. He then lay back down with the young lion and held him close once more.

Soon after, he went to sleep as well, with a lion in his arms...and in his heart.

Secret Punishment
New Jersey, United States - 1918 CE

I had no idea where I was, unable to see anything due to the sack over my head. However, I felt sore from the beating before we arrived. I was moved into a chair that reeked of cigarette smoke. If my hooves weren't tied, I would've taken the sack off my head and looked around with my good eye, since my other was blackened from the beating. Someone soon removed it and untied the rope that bound my hooves.

I looked around, and found myself in a small, mysterious, dimly lit room. I was sitting at one end of a long table. On the other end was a green iguana wearing a fur coat, who I assumed was the don. To either side of the table were two other men in suits. I could smell hair gel as one of the men slicked his hair back. All of them looked at least 30 years old. One of the men, a lion, gave a smirk as he took in my swollen eye and bloody face. I looked to either side of me and saw bulls standing with their arms crossed.

There weren't many sounds, just the occasional cough or shifting of chairs. I didn't know whether to be scared, but I knew I was confused. On the table I saw a note with the bearing of a saint-like figure on it, a dagger, and a pistol. As confused as I was, I imagined that I knew what this was about.

"Diego Luca Martin Rosato," said the iguana. I was sure I knew what this was about, now that he had said my name. I took my chances by speaking.

"What are you—"

"Quiet, sheep!" shouted the bull behind me as he forcefully put his hoof on my shoulder. "No talking while the don is talking."

"Easy, Enzo," the lizard said as he put his hand up. "He's good people—or so I hope. You may call me Vinny, and I will call you Marty." He turned toward a cat who I knew personally. The feline nodded back at him. It surprised me to see him here.

"Sorry, boss," the bull replied as he removed his hoof from my shoulder.

"You see here, Marty," Vinny leaned back in his chair, "I don't let just anyone into the father's family." I stayed silent as he continued. "Now, Marty, how committed would you be to the family?" He took out a needle and passed it to one of the bulls. "Now, you may speak."

"I'm very loyal, sir," I replied with a stern, stoic demeanor. "I'm no songbird."

"Good answer," he said with a smirk. "How do you feel about rigging? How do you feel about whacking someone?"

"If someone thinks they can get away with crossing a crime family, they have it coming." I shrugged.

He let out a bellowing laugh and slammed his hand on the table.

"Sounds a lot like my father!" he said. "Never liked him, but he's right. Johnny." He snapped his fingers at the other bull next to me.

The bull gave me the needle. I looked at it, then at Vinny.

"You are to prick your finger and drip drops of blood onto the saint," he said as he leaned over the table.

I did as he asked. The needle went deep into my finger, making me wince. I squeezed my finger and spilled a few drops of blood onto the drawing of the saint. Johnny gave me a tissue for my finger as the others passed the paper back to Vinny. He took a small cylindrical block and smeared the blood over the drawing. He held up the blood-stained saint in front of me.

"See this?" he asked. "If you betray D'onofrio," he continued, slowly ripping the bloody drawing in half. "You'll end up just like this saint, capisce?"

I looked at the men on each side of the table, then nodded at Vinny.

"Good, now get outta here." Joseph waved his hand. The big horned guys put the sack back over my head and picked me up by my arms. Knowing that the mafia had some sort of code of silence, it seemed reasonable, so I didn't resist.

They carried me out of the room. Where I was going, I didn't know. I soon found myself tossed into what I figured was a car or a van. They tied my hooves again. I heard the engine start. Seeing as I had nowhere to go and I was already in the position for it, I decided to take a nap.

The vehicle's abrupt stop woke me up and slammed me into the seat in front of me. I was then carried out and placed onto my foot hooves. All I could hear was more indistinct chatter and vehicles passing by. I felt the cold chill of the wind blowing on my arms.

I was then rushed into a more quiet area; no more cars or indistinct chatter could be heard. As I was led by the men, I heard a door open. Finally, the cold wind abandoned me as we entered a warm room. The door slammed behind me, and my mask was untied and snatched from my head. I looked around and saw a hall leading to stairs that went down. Behind me, I saw Vinny and Enzo towering over me.

"Come on, sheep," Enzo said as he pushed my back. "Let's get this over with."

"You have such a good way with people, Enzo," Johnny replied and gave a sigh. "Be more subtle, less aggressive and bullheaded."

"You're very funny, Johnny," Enzo said, then snorted.

As we went down the stairs, I started to hear trumpet music. At the bottom of the steps, I saw what looked like a small pub. People dressed very casually. They played pool, poker, and craps. The black cat who was at the meeting greeted me, and the two bulls left my side.

"It's good to see you, Charlie," I greeted the cat as we shook hands.

"Good to see you, too, Marty," he replied, "Don't think you're out of the fire yet, though. You're under my watch."

"What does that mean?" I crossed my arms and looked around curiously.

"It means what I said. You're now a soldier, and I'm your boss, I guess you could say. Don't worry though; you're free to do what you want, as long as you follow our code."

"Which is…?"

Charlie took me into a small, dark room and turned on a light. On the back wall was a sheet of paper with a list on it.

"These are the ten commandments of a Mafioso, my friend. This list is what we go by. This is our bible." He pointed to the first commandment. "Read it."

"No one can present himself directly to another of our friends," I read, squinting at the small print. "There must be a third person to do it." Being in the family, I already knew what this meant. I heard Charlie give a chuckle. "Never look at the wives of friends."

"I shouldn't have to explain that to you, right Marty?" He crossed his arms. "That would probably get you in trouble not just here, but outside the family as well." He chuckled. "Next."

"Never be seen with cops," I continued.

"Even silver-tongued men can trip themselves up." He leaned against the wall and shook his head. "It's best to not take any chances."

"Don't go to pubs and clubs."

"The don is pretty lax on this one, actually," he said with a chuckle. "He frequents the ladies at clubs himself; he don't got a wife to go home to. What's the next one?"

"Your number one priority is to the D'onofrio Family…" I raised an eyebrow and looked at him, "Even if your wife is…giving birth?"

"Even if your wife is giving birth, even if your child is deathly ill, or even if you yourself are sick, you always be available for the family, you hear? She don't need your help pushing the kid out." When I heard that, my heart skipped a beat—and not in the good way. He gave me a stern look. "We are your family now, Marty," he said as he put his hand on my shoulder. "What do families do? They look out for each other. You look out for us, we'll look out for you. Don't worry—it's not as bad as it sounds. The rest are pretty self-explanatory."

"As your superiors, appointments must be respected," I continued. "Wives must be treated with respect." I saw some handwriting after that rule. "Unless…unless she disrespects you. Ha! Good one. If money doesn't belong to you, you aren't allowed to appropriate it. People who can't be part of D'onofrio: anyone who has a close relative in the police, anyone with a two-timing relative in the family, anyone who displays bad behavior, and anyone who doesn't hold to moral values."

"Understand those rules, Marty," he said with a nod. "You're under my watch. Don't think you can shirk these rules just because we're friends. I put the family first. Now get outta here."

He opened the door and let me out.

In the next few months I became accustomed to how things worked in the family. I became more of a soldier. I knew how to rig horse races, fix fights and championships, and even helped Charlie whack a guy.

I didn't notice the perks going to my head. I started to be cockier—even more bullheaded than Enzo.

My cockiness caught up to me when I found myself drunk and in the bed of Small Paul's wife, Angela, or Angie as the others call her. Small Paul was the don's son. I was at a pub because I found my wife cheating on another sheep. Angie bought me a few drinks. We talked, laughed, and kissed at times. She talked about how Small Paul became less pleasing to her—he was more obnoxious and angry as years went by, like any Italian gator would be.

The next thing I knew, I was in the mouse's bed, both of us naked, and me on top of her. I quickly got up and grabbed my clothing from the chair beside the bed.

"Good morning, handsome," she said as I saw her lean up on the bed. She gave me a coy smile. "Leaving so soon?"

"Y-yeah," I replied. I had to choose my words carefully, as I knew I was walking through a minefield now. "Have you seen my underclothes?"

"You mean these?" She lifted up the bed sheets and revealed that she was wearing them, and only them. "You can have them back."

"Err, it's okay. Keep them." I started to put my clothes on. "I should get going. Last night was...nice."

"Must it end?" She got up and grabbed my arm. "Can't we have another wonderful time?"

"We weren't even supposed to have it this time, Angie," I replied as I snatched my arm away and finished getting dressed.

"So you're just going to leave me like this?"

"You have a husband, Angie! And I have...or had, a wife. The point is, we shouldn't have done this. Now I gotta go before Small Paul gets back." I headed for the door.

"He doesn't treat me nice anymore, Marty! You can't just push me aside like he does!"

"I'm sorry, Angie," I replied, "I shouldn't have done this."

"Fine... and I won't tell Small Paul. I guess I should thank you for this. It felt...great."

I closed the door behind me. I left her house and sighed.

I had already broken two of the commandments: interacting with another man's wife, and going to a pub. In hopes of hiding all of this, I stayed clear of any of the family members and Angie for a week. I only went back to the mafia home after I thought the incident was swept under the rug.

When I returned, I saw some of the family members standing on either side of the hallway. They gave me nasty glares. I walked by Charlie as he sighed and shook his head.

"You're in trouble, kid," he whispered.

There's no way they could've found out, I thought. I figured that someone would have said something by then, right? I went down the stairs into the room where more men were lined up as though they were directing me. The line led to the don's room. I knew now for sure that they knew. One of the members opened the door for me as I walked in, and slammed the door behind me.

"Sit down, Luca," Vinny said, with the back of his chair facing me. Enzo stood to the side of me in a suit, with his arms crossed. I sat in the chair in front of his desk.

"Luca," he said. "We're a family, are we not?" He slowly turned around to face me with a cigar in his mouth. "We look out for each other, right?"

"Yeah, boss. I—"

"You talk when I tell you." He blew out a ring of smoke. "Angie came by the other day. She was in tears. She was talking about how you supposedly raped and abused her. Don't worry though." He chuckled. "Broad's a terrible liar. However, I do know you slept with her. Word gets around like schoolgirls in this family." He put his arms on the desk and leaned in. "Did you really think I wouldn't find out? Now you can talk."

"It's not what it looks like, boss,"

"You kiddin' me? You sleep with my son's wife—my son's wife! You go to the pubs. You lie about it to Enzo, and now you're trying to lie to me?"

I looked over at Enzo as he snorted and gave me the same glare as the others.

"Look, Marty. You're a good kid, and I like ya." The smile on his face made me think he would let me off easily. "But you're getting a big head. You're getting full of yourself." He turned his chair back around, facing the picture of his father on the wall. "You need to be reminded who's in charge, kid. No hard feelings."

Enzo cracked his knuckles and gave me a menacing grin. He walked closer to me, his golden eyes twinkling.

"W-wait, you're gonna beat me up?" I asked, looking up at the bull.

"Not exactly," Vinny replied. "You broke one of our rules, so we're gonna break you. Like I said—no hard feelings. I just can't have any funny business in the family."

The bull dropped his pants and I saw his huge bulge as if it was staring me down. Before I knew it, was grabbed out of the chair, and my pants were ripped off.

"Wait, what!?" I exclaimed as I stepped back. Enzo grabbed my arm and slammed me over the desk. "I'm not..."

"You brought this on yourself, Marty," Vinny replied. "I wish I could say I'm sorry, but... well, you broke the rules."

The big bull grabbed my small horns. I squirmed and whimpered softly as he tugged at my tail.

"Oh relax, it doesn't last that long," Vinny said. Enzo snorted angrily at Vinny's remark.

The bull slammed my head on the desk. All I could see was the wall and the desk. I then felt something throb against my bare behind.

"Wait," I said, "I don't want..."

"Should've followed the rules then," Enzo replied. I felt his huge member prodding my hole. "Mmm, nice and tight. This is gonna be good."

He proceeded to shove his thick cock into my hole. I gritted my teeth and fought tears as he went deeper. It felt like he was tearing my insides.

"That hurts!" I yelled. "S-stop, please!" I felt tears running down my face. It felt like the more I whimpered and cried, the harder he went. "No! That—" As I was about to cry out again, I felt him hit a spot inside me. It made me moan, and my own cock throb.

"You're not enjoying this, are you, sheep?"

"N-no!" I responded. "Let me go!" I stifled my moans, biting on my hoof. If they found out, something worse might happen.

As I tried to look up, I caught a glance of smoke; most likely Vinny enjoying his cigar. There was no point in struggling, Enzo was bigger and stronger than me and could probably snap my neck if he had a mind to. Although, it would probably be less painful if he did.

The thought of that vile woman, Angie, ran through my mind: "I have needs," she had said. "You can't just leave me like this!" Then she had screamed and thrown a vase at me before I left. If that was the way she treated Small Paul, then no wonder he became distant.

The bull smacked me in the back of the head, knocking me back into reality.

"What are you sleeping or something?" Enzo asked. "I want to hear you fucking bleat, you little bastard! Bleat!" he chanted as he continued to smack me around.

"Please stop! It hurts!" I lied as I pounded my fist on the table and he pounded into me. I bit my lower lip, my eyes half-closed, trying not to look like I was having fun too. He pulled me up by my horns as I helplessly gazed at the back of the boss's chair.

Enzo got close to my ear and licked my cheek. His member pulsated even harder inside me. It was as though he enjoyed me trembling in fear and feeling so much pain, though I was actually trembling in pleasure.

"I'll stop when I'm good and finished," he whispered in my ear as he held me against him. I could feel his sweat spill through his clothes onto my back. I also felt his hot breath on my neck as he panted heavily. "Here it comes." I felt a wave of his thick seed flowing inside of me, as though I had just been impregnated. He snorted loudly against my neck and wrapped his arms tightly around me.

I felt lightheaded from the pounding that he had given me. The last thing I heard was Vinny, who said, "Get him on his back." I then drifted in and out of consciousness.

"He's a real good kid, ain't he, Enzo?" I heard Vinny's voice. I slowly woke up to see Vinny's giant green lizard member and Enzo's brown bull cock towering over me. I then noticed that I was stripped bare. As I tried to move, I saw that my arms and legs were restrained by ropes. They both looked down at me with sinister grins, their meat in hand as they started jerking.

"I'm sure Charlie told you about that rule where you can't go to pubs," Vinny said. "And he probably told you about how I got no wife, eh Luca?" I looked up at both of them, pretending to struggle to break free. "This is why, kid. Handsome little cocky brats like you that want to be rule breakers. Though I'm not that disrespectful; that's Enzo."

"Please, just let me go," I whimpered.

"Keep whining like that. Enzo likes it," Vinny said, and chuckled. I figured he liked hearing other people's "pain."

Before long, they both climaxed all over me. The smell and feel of their seed on my body made me feel dirty and violated. I laid there lifeless, feeling broken and destroyed.

"Enzo, get him cleaned up and dressed. Luca," I stared blankly at the ceiling as Enzo untied me from the ropes. "You didn't see nothing, you hear?" He grabbed my face. "Nothing. Now get 'em outta here."

Enzo hoisted me up and took me into a bathroom to get me cleaned up. He put my clothes back on me, as I continued to stare blankly with a faint smile on my face.

"Hey," Enzo said. "Hey!" he slapped me and grabbed my face. I snapped back into reality and looked at him. "You didn't see nothing. I know the boss said it, but me? I'm telling you. Got it? Boss's family is my family. You do anything to jeopardize that, and I'll break you even more."

He let me go as I stood up. I limped back into the office with my head down in false shame. I looked over at the don, now fully dressed again.

"Stand up straight, kid," he said as he folded his hands on his desk. "You didn't see a thing, and that means you didn't feel a thing either, got it?" I would've disagreed with not feeling anything, but I didn't want to get into more "trouble." I struggled, but managed to stand up normally. "You remember that, and you'll be fine. This'll be the only time you can lie about something. Don't let me catch you breaking the rules again." I nodded at him and turned around. "And Luca?" I looked back at him. "Keep a pressure check on that big head of yours." He started smoking another cigar.

If that was the punishment for breaking the rules, I wouldn't mind being the cocky little brat he said I was.

After the Match
Guadalajara, Mexico - 1963 CE

As the wrestler bounced around the ring, he took off his hooded jacket, revealing his brown ponytail and slender figure. He tossed the jacket to his burly bear of a manager, who stood outside the ring.

"I love you, Tornado!" shouted one of the spectators.

Tornado crouched down, stretching out his legs as his squirrel tail swayed. Looking at the audience, he lifted his arms as they cheered for him.

The lights beamed toward the entrance, revealing a fennec fox just as small and fit as the squirrel. A taller vixen accompanied him, wearing a silver low-cut dress. As his opponent made his way down the aisle, his silver mask and pants shining in the light, his blue eyes peered at the light blue mask Tornado wore. Hearing the audience cheer put a smile on the fox's face.

The fox vaulted over the ropes into the ring and fixed his mask. As the two wrestlers approached each other, they butted heads until the referee sent them to opposite corners. The arena lit up again, showing the spectators cheering and holding up signs.

The ring announcer stepped forward.

"In this corner," he said, pointing to the squirrel, "From Guadalajara, Mexico, weighing in at 62 kilograms, the number one contender for the World Lightweight Championship: Timo

Tornado!" The crowd cheered loudly as Tornado raised his arms.

"And his opponent, from Buenos Aires, Argentina," he pointed to the fox, "Weighing in at 61 kilograms, and nine-time World Lightweight Champion: Claudio Ciclón!" The crowd cheered again as Ciclón raised his own arms.

The referee pointed to each of them, and they responded with a nod. He then pointed to the bell ringer outside the ring.

The bell was rung and the match began. The two squared off, circling each other. After eyeing each other for a few seconds, they clashed in a struggling grapple, each trying to gain the upper hand. The squirrel then wrapped his arms around his opponent, and tossed him over his hip.

Looking up at the squirrel, Ciclón rolled backward and hopped back up. With a few kicks, punches, and misses, the two backed away from each other. As usual, Ciclón turned to the crowd and showed off, rousing the spectators.

Hearing them cheer for his opponent, Tornado posed as well, turning toward the crowd and raising his arms. Cheers came from his fans as well. The two wrestlers turned toward each other, competing for the crowd's favor. The audience soon started chanting their names.

Staring each other down, they charged and clashed again. This time the fennec tossed the squirrel into the ropes. As the blue masked fighter bounced off them and ran toward his opponent, the fox retaliated with a dropkick to the chest, sending Tornado out of the ring.

As the squirrel stood up, disoriented, he glanced at the ring to see Ciclón fly out of the ring and crash into him. They fell into the unguarded crowd, though refrained from knocking anyone over; the younger female looked excited to be a momentary part of the action. The two wrestlers moved to reenter the ring, gradually regaining most of their composure.

Still dazed, Tornado charged at Ciclón, but the quick fox dodged, and the squirrel landed in the corner. Ciclón held the squirrel against the corner with his hand and gave a swift chop to his chest. The painful smacking sound made the crowd gasp.

The fox wound up and gave another chop to the chest before letting go.

Holding his torso, Tornado panted and managed to move away from his opponent. As he turned around, he saw the fox running at him, and retaliated with a clothesline, knocking Ciclón down.

Chuckling at the downed fox the squirrel climbed to the top rope and gestured to the crowd again, listening to them cheer. He performed a front flip onto Ciclón and pinning his shoulders down.

The referee scurried over to them and hit the mat as he counted: One, the audience joined in, two. The fox managed to kick his way out of the pin, however, and stop the count.

The two leaped to their feet and clashed again, each trying to gain the advantage. Blow for blow and throw for throw, they seemed evenly matched. Matches were not supposed to last too long, but seeing how excited the audience was, the two dragged it out just for show.

Ciclón grabbed Tornado's arm and swung him into the ring post. On the other side of the ring, his vixen could be seen cheering. She blew a kiss at the fox, and he caught it with his hand, smiling at her. He then focused on the hurt squirrel, dragging him back into the ring.

Pounding on the mat could be heard from Tornado's manager. "Get up, hombre!" he said.

Tornado slowly got to his feet. Anticipating the clothesline that Ciclón was about to deliver, the squirrel ducked behind him, grabbed his waist, and pinned him with a suplex.

With the fox's shoulders down, the referee began to count. However, before he got to two, Ciclón's manager approached the outside of the ring as if she was about to get in. Shouting and pointing, she distracted the referee. He walked over to her, arguing and telling her to get off the apron. The audience booed and hissed at her. At the same time, Ciclón escaped the pin and hit Tornado with his signature move, a jumping kick to his opponent's head, knocking him down again. He raised a fist to the crowd, hearing them cheer and boo. He then turned the semiconscious squirrel onto his back and prepared for his finishing move. He raised both of his hands then ran toward the ropes, springing off the top rope while doing a twisting moonsault. Before he could land, Tornado rolled out the way, causing the fox to land hard on his back.

Seeing her wrestler in pain, Ciclón's manager started pounding on the mat herself. As she got up on the apron again, Tornado's manager carried her off as to not cause any more distractions. The audience cheered for the manager holding her back.

As the fox got back up he was clearly dazed, facing away from the squirrel. Tornado turned him around and performed his finisher: a twisting DDT. He pinned the fox's shoulders and the referee counted: One...two...three. The bell rang and the crowd cheered.

"And the winner and the new World Lightweight Champion," said the announcer, "Tooornadooo!"

The crowd cheered as Tornado was handed the belt. His manager entered the ring and gave him a big bear hug, holding the squirrel's arm up in victory.

In the locker room, Tornado looked at the championship belt around his waist: "FWF" in big crimson letters on a gold background and "World Lightweight Champion" on the border. He took it off and smiled, kissing it before putting it on the bench.

Undressing, he put a towel around his waist. As he turned around, he bumped into Ciclón, who was also in a towel.

"Are you done ogling that thing, Timoteo?" he asked. "Or shall I give you more time alone?" He crossed his arms and smirked.

"Upset that someone beat your streak, Claudio?"

They went into the small open showers and removed their towels. The sound of running water echoed throughout the room.

"Upset? Why would I be? If anyone were to beat my streak, I'd rather it be my former tag partner." The fox grabbed a bar of soap and started lathering himself. "Besides, I'm glad that match was over. That finisher hurt."

"I suppose you have a point," the squirrel replied as he washed himself. "I did miss those days teaming up with you." He accidentally dropped the soap. As he bent over, Claudio subtly glanced at the squirrel's butt and raised tail.

"I won't argue there." The fox reached out and began washing Timo's back. "And don't forget our little agreement, Timo."

"Right now?" Timo asked as he looked at Claudio. "But—"

"Remember? You said anytime I'm interested." He wrapped his arms around the squirrel, massaging his torso. "Besides, who could look at that rump and not be excited?"

"Coming from a fox?" Timo rubbed his butt against Claudio's groin, then turned around and grinned at him. "How long has it been since we've teamed up like this?"

"Too long, my friend." He kissed the squirrel, his hands on his rear as their sheaths pressed together. "Too long. Do you remember what I said about our deal?" He saw a red mark on the squirrel's chest. "Did I hit you too hard?" His ears flattened.

Timo shook his head and smiled. "We've both had worse, Claudio. Nothing to be worried about." He kissed the fox and rubbed his back. At the same time, Claudio rubbed his hands over the squirrel's butt, murring and sliding his tongue inside Timo's mouth.

The squirrel broke the kiss and glanced to the side. "Just...be gentle. We've never done it that way before."

Claudio held him close, their damp fur pressing together. "Not to worry, partner. I know you'll enjoy it."

"How long do you think we'll be able to continue like this, Claudio?" He gazed into the fox's blue eyes.

"What do you mean? I guess we would keep going until...you know," Claudio replied with a wink, rubbing along the squirrel's toned chest and flat stomach, making Timo gasp. As the fox's hand slid lower, Timo stopped him.

"I mean your manager, Claudio. Angela?" He lowered his gaze to the running water.

"I don't see her around." His eyes darted from left to right.

"Do you, Timo?" He wrapped his arms around the squirrel again, kissing his muzzle.

"I...suppose you have a point." The squirrel blushed as he looked at the fox's slender but toned figure.

"My lips are sealed." He walked Timo over to the wall, pinning his shoulders. "Enough about her, though. Now it's just you and me. Show me that you deserve that belt."

The fox held his arms above his head, opening his mouth and pressing it against the squirrel's neck. He sucked gently so as not to leave a mark. Their sheaths grinding together, Timo felt his cock emerging as he released a shaky breath. They kissed deeply, pressing their tongues to one another.

Claudio placed his hands on Timo's firm rump. Feeling those hands made the squirrel weak in the knees. As they kissed, the fox reached down to stroke their cocks as they fully emerged from their sheaths.

After they parted lips, Claudio got onto his knees and licked up the length of the squirrel's pink cock, already leaking pre-cum from his pleasure. Just to tease more, he fondled Timo's balls, causing him to murr and throb more. After having his fun, Claudio looked at the squirrel's cock with hungry eyes and wrapped his muzzle around it, making the swollen length almost disappear into his maw.

His knees buckling, Timo could only lean against the wall. He rubbed the fox's head and pushed forward, making him take his cock faster. With a groan, he let go of the fox but began thrusting into his maw, his erection leaking pre-cum. He felt Claudio's tongue sliding over his throbbing member.

The heady scent of their arousals filled the room as Timo clawed at the concrete shower wall. He groaned as he felt his climax growing near. Thrusting faster, Timo hovered on the edge of release. He growled as he released his spunk into Claudio's muzzle. Drinking load after load, the fox could not take anymore and pulled the squirrel's small cock out of his mouth, letting some of the cum hit his face. As Timo looked at the fox's dripping muzzle, he pulled him up for a kiss, savoring the taste of his own spunk.

"Your seed tastes as good as ever, Timo." Claudio smiled and pulled him close, kissing him deeply. He cupped his hands around the squirrel's butt and looked at him with half-lidded eyes. "Now it's my turn, partner." He grinned and picked the squirrel up, Timo's legs wrapped around Claudio's waist.

The fox started thrusting against Timo, sliding his member between the squirrel's cheeks. As they kissed, Claudio slipped a finger inside the squirrel's hole and thrust it slowly within him. Timo winced as the finger moved inside his tight passage.

"Just relax, Timo," the fox said, nuzzling his chin. "It will feel better soon."

The squirrel felt Claudio's hard cock against his entrance. Even though he wasn't large, Timo's tight hole made up for that.

He lifted the flexible squirrel's leg up over his shoulder. Timo let out a loud moan as he felt the fox's cock penetrate him. The squirrel pounded his fist against the wall and clenched his teeth. Claudio groaned as he pushed deeper into Timo's body, panting and sweating.

"You feel so warm, Timo." He leaned in, slipping his tongue inside the squirrel's maw and making out with him again. Claudio groaned into the kiss as he began to thrust into the squirrel's rear.

As Claudio pumped into him, Timo wrapped his arms around the fox's neck as his cock grew hard against Claudio's abs. He wrapped his legs around his waist again.

"I see you are enjoying this more than you expected," said the fox as he began stroking Timo's cock. The squirrel's sensitive shaft twitched and throbbed at his touch. To arouse him even more, Claudio began sucking and licking at one of Timo's nipples, making the squirrel gasp and moan. "I always love hearing you make that sound." He continued teasing the squirrel.

Claudio gradually picked up the pace, thrusting harder and deeper, and panting as he pressed against the squirrel. He groaned as he grew close to his release. Claudio's stroking of his member had Timo nearing a second climax.

Claudio thrusted quicker, hilting into the squirrel with each thrust. His arousal at a peak, he hugged onto Timo and groaned in pleasure.

Timo moaned out, as he shot thick ropes of his hot seed all over the fennec and himself. Feeling the squirrel cum all over him, Claudio released his spunk inside Timo, moaning out and panting as he turned around and leaned against the wall.

Claudio pulled out of the squirrel and kissed his cheek. Timo kept his legs wrapped around the fox's waist, panting against his neck. Claudio soon lowered him to his feet. The squirrel's legs felt weak; however, he wobbled as he tried to stand. The fox supported him and kissed his cheek.

"Let me know if you need me to throw another match for you," Claudio said, smiling at the squirrel.

"I wouldn't mind teaming up with you again. The Typhoon could reunite." He winked at the fox and chuckled.

"That sounds like a good idea, amigo."

As they shared one more kiss, the championship belt was stolen by a familiar manager. A feminine giggle could be heard in the locker room.

"Did you hear something?" asked Timo.

"What is it?" Claudio looked around the showers, but saw nobody.

"Never mind. Now, where were we?" Timo smiled and started making out with his partner again.

www.ingramcontent.com/pod-product-compliance
Lightning Source LLC
Chambersburg PA
CBHW061206170626
46809CB00003B/1268

* 9 7 8 1 9 4 5 2 4 7 0 5 7 *